Rescue

Horse

An Inspirational Horse Show Adventure Series

for Horse Crazy Girls

High Lane Farm 1

Shannon Jett

To my Mom and Dad, for accepting that I was horse crazy and loving me anyway. And for Lolly, who is my Arwen.

Chapter 1

Shelby carefully removed the leather bridle from the bridle hook and threw the reins over her shoulder. She shook off her gloves, stuffing them in her coat pocket and winced as she grasped the bit in her hands. She paced around the tack room for several minutes, warming the metal in her hands, before heading out the door where her horse, Arwen was waiting.

"Sorry for the wait, but I didn't think you'd want me shoving a cold bit in your mouth."

Shelby expertly bridled the horse and headed toward the mounting block. The sun was quickly fading, but Shelby knew she still had plenty of time for a quick ride.

Shelby was determined to ride as much as possible, even if it meant saddling up on brisk days. The Rivermont Farm Silver Stirrup Series was rapidly approaching and Shelby's trainer had finally allowed her to move up to the 2'6" hunter division.

Arwen danced around as the leaves circled under her feet. Shelby talked softly to the mare and she quieted quickly. Shelby was so grateful for the bond she shared with the bay mare. Many people claimed Arabians to be flighty and spirited, but Shelby believed they were just sensitive and smart. Shelby had been riding Arwen for about six months and they had clicked instantly.

Shelby was trotting along when she noticed her trainer, Allison High, standing by the gate.

"If all of my students were as dedicated as you are, High Lane Farm would be undefeated!" Allison said as Shelby trotted over.

"How's our girl?" she asked Shelby as she absentmindedly stroked the mare's forehead.

"A little jazzed up, but she's listening well."

"I made Chelsea ride her in a lesson the other day."

"How did it go?" Shelby asked hesitantly.

Chelsea was a good rider and was starting to shop for a horse of her very own. Even though Arwen was a lesson horse at High Lane Farm,

Shleby always felt like the mare was her own. Not too many of the other students got along with her as well as Shelby, so she wasn't usually a favorite for lessons. Luckily, Allison felt the mare was very talented and a great match for Shelby so she didn't mind keeping her around even though she wasn't really pulling her weight as a lesson horse.

"It went about as you would expect. Chelsea did a good job with her, but Arwen definitely kept her on her toes. Such a mare!" She looked up at Shelby and burst out laughing. "You should see your face! You look so worried! Don't panic, no one is taking your girl away from you. Besides, Chelsea is going to need something taller."

Shelby breathed a sigh of relief. She liked Chelsea and knew the older girl was excited to be getting a horse for her birthday, but she couldn't help being relieved that it wouldn't be her Arwen. She was counting on their partnership to earn them top honors at the Rivermont Shows. Perhaps they would even be contenders for the overall circuit Division Championships!

"Well, I better get back to it if I want to finish anytime soon. Maybe I could talk you into helping when you are done?" Allison hinted slyly.

"Of course," Shelby smiled. She loved doing barn chores. She loved every minute she could spend at the stable. "Be there in a minute."

As she went back to practicing her sitting trot, Shelby was glad for the chance to ride with a trainer like Allison who thoroughly believed in her and let her work off lessons and extra ride time by helping with barn chores. Her parents were supportive of her riding habit, but didn't quite understand the obsession. And they definitely didn't have the money to pay for unlimited riding and lessons.

When she felt like they had reached a good stopping point, Shelby opened her fingers and let the reins slide through them as Arwen stretched her nose to the ground. She scratched the horse's withers as she cooled her down. The sun was setting and the temperature was quickly dropping. Shelby dismounted and headed to the well-lit, warm stable.

After Arwen was untacked and brushed down, Shelby led the bay mare back to her stall. As soon as she shut the stall door, Arwen thrust her head over the door demanding dinner.

"In a minute, lady!" Shelby told her stroking the blaze on the center of her face. Arwen shoved at her impatiently so Shelby moved on to start being helpful.

High Lane Farm was a small barn that specialized in Arabians and Half- Arabians. Allison taught many lessons, beginner through advanced in both dressage and jumping. Their barn was small by many standards, only eight stalls, but Shelby loved how well all of the students knew each other and the horses. It was like a big family.

The number of horses at the farm varied, as is usual with many busy stables. The main barn was always full and then there were several large pastures with roomy run-in sheds to accommodate the horses that lived outside. There was a large, lighted outdoor arena, a smaller grass area that was good for schooling and the farm property backed up to a forest with tons of well- kept trails. High Lane Farm was heaven for Shelby.

After tucking all the horses in for the night, Shelby sat down with Allison in her office to wait for her mom to pick her up.

"Can I ride Arwen tomorrow?" she asked.

Allison glanced at her calendar on the wall. "I've actually scheduled a lesson with Chelsea and I'd like for her to ride Arwen again."

She continued, "I've found a horse that I think will be a good match for Chelsea, but he's a bit more...er....cantankerous than the school horses she is used to riding. She is definitely ready to move up to a horse that's a little classier, she just needs to build her confidence on a horse that's not completely push button. She and I both agree that riding Arwen for a few weeks will be good practice for her. But you are welcomed to come out! I'm sure I can find something for you to do and Chelsea might appreciate some tips."

Shelby wasn't sure she would. Chelsea was three years older than her, the same age as Shelby's older sister, Sage. She tried to imagine giving Sage advice. She didn't think it would go over well!

"Hey Tucker, my man!" Allison exclaimed as Shelby's mom and ten year old brother walked through the door. She gave him a high five and grinned at Shelby's mom.

"Hey guys!" Shelby's mom said cheerily. "How was your ride?" she asked Shelby.

Shelby's mom knew nothing about horses, but she'd always let Shelby prattle on about them and act interested. She was also famous at the barn for fixing the most amazing horse show lunches. No one from High Lane Farm went hungry.

"Pretty good," Shelby said as she gathered up her things to get ready to leave. "Cold, though."

"Allison, thanks so much for everything you do for her. Shelby's lucky to have you."

"Well, she's a bit of a pain but I guess it's no big deal," Allison replied winking at Shelby. "No. I'm lucky to have her. She's great help."

"We better get a move on. Sage and your Dad are home starting dinner and I hate to think of them burning down the house."

Chapter 2

Shelby walked into the barn the next day after school. Her friend Taylor was supposed to meet her after she finished with a dentist appointment.

"Shelby! I'm so glad to see you!" a voice exclaimed from a stall. Chelsea stood up from wrapping Arwen's legs. "You can give me some pointers on this lady here," she said pointing at Arwen.

Shelby was thrilled that the older girl was asking for advice. "Yeah, Allison told me you were riding her for a few weeks. How is it going?"

"Thanks for being so cool about it. It's going ok, I guess. I definitely have lots to figure out. But it's good for me to have to push myself a little. Did Allison tell you why?" Chelsea's eyes danced.

"She mentioned the possibility of finding a good match for you."

"Shelby, I'm so excited! I just want to ride him perfectly when we go see him. I'm already calling him mine. Isn't that awful? I'm just so excited and I hope it works out. Want to see a picture?"

She grabbed her phone and thumbed through the saved photos stopping on a picture of a handsome chestnut with four white socks.

"He's lovely!" Shelby acknowledged. "So flashy! What's his name?"

"Socks," she groaned. "Kinda dorky, but cute, too. His show name is CA Business Socks."

"Oh, I like it. Where is he?"

"He's at Glenn Lake Farm. Apparently his owner doesn't get along with him and told the trainer to sell him right away."

"Very fancy!" Shelby exclaimed.

Glenn Lake was a big time show barn about two hours away. They competed at all the big rated shows and always had several National winners. Allison tried to make it up there to ride with their head trainer, John DeMarc, whenever she could and he would frequently let her know if a good deal came along.

"I know, right! Now I just hope I can ride him. So, back to Arwen. When I warmed her up last time I tried lots of bending, but it just seemed to aggravate her."

"She hates bending. She hates warming up. Seriously. The most effective thing I have found is to walk her on a loose rein for a few minutes then long trot her around the arena a few times. Then she'll be ready to go to work for you, and you can collect her up and bend her all you want. But if you try to do that before she's had her little romp, she gets grumpy."

"Good to know!" Chelsea laughed.

"She's a bit of a diva," Shelby cooed into Arwen's ear. "But she's a pretty girl."

"That she is. Really beautiful. Well, I better get on down to the arena to start our warm up process. Thanks for the tips!"

Shelby watched Chelsea lead Arwen down the barn aisle.

"Quit mooning over that horse!" joked a voice behind her.

"Taylor, you're here!" Shelby greeted her friend. Taylor and Shelby had become best friends after bonding over their lack of coordination in fifth grade gym class. Three years later they were still uncoordinated but shared an incredible friendship and love of horses. Taylor had started taking riding lessons a year and a half ago after much prodding from Shelby. She quickly realized she was a natural and she was completely horse crazy. The girls often felt like they spent more time together at the barn than they spent anywhere else and they wouldn't have it any other way.

"How long have we got?" Shelby asked. Taylor's mom was picking the girls up and taking them back to Taylor's house to work on a school project.

"Mom said she'd be back in an hour. So... an hour and fifteen minutes," Taylor grinned. Her mom was notoriously late.

"Good," Allison said walking up to them. "I can use some help. Could you load about ten of the extra buckets in the feed room into the back of my truck?"

"Sure, what for?" Taylor asked.

"My friend Judy, that runs Hoofed Hearts Equine Rescue called and they just got in a few more rescue horses and need to borrow some buckets. I'm dropping them off after lessons. Thanks girls."

Taylor and Shelby headed to the feed room to pull out the buckets. Allison was incredibly organized and very picky about the cleanliness of her stable. So it was no surprise to the girls to find several tidy stacks of buckets in the corner of the room. They each took a stack and placed them in the truck before returning to the barn.

"Now what?" Shelby asked. Neither girl liked to sit idle in the barn. Not that it happened often. There was far too much to do.

"I promised Allison I would pull Mercury's mane." Taylor responded. "Want to hold him while I do the top?"

Taylor was an expert mane puller. She was very careful and precise, and none of the horses seemed to mind when she did it.

Mercury was a half Arab, half Welsh pony used for lessons. He was a kind, gentle pony responsible for helping many riders get their start.

Taylor found a stool while Shelby pulled Mercury out of his stall. It was easier to have someone hold him while Taylor worked on the top part of his mane to keep him from fidgeting.

"Have you ever been to the rescue?" Taylor asked Shelby.

"Once, about a year ago. She didn't have too many horses there at the time. Allison said it has really grown lately, which is sad, I guess. Rescue is probably one of those things you hope doesn't grow."

"Too many people not taking care of their horses. It's so sad," Taylor replied quietly. "I'd want to bring them all home with me."

"Ha, ha! Allison would kill us!" Shelby scratched Mercury's neck to keep him steady as Taylor worked her way down the mane.

"We'll get ya all prettied up, you handsome boy." she whispered.

"I'm at a good spot where you could tie him up now if you want." Taylor said to Shelby. "I know you are probably dying to watch the last bit of Arwen's ride."

"I am! You don't mind?" she asked Taylor. Taylor shook her head and Shelby scurried out into the sunlight and toward the arena.

Chapter 3

Shelby watched as Chelsea gracefully piloted the mare through a serpentine pattern. The mare looked calm and relaxed, as did the rider. Shelby might be worried that Chelsea would fall in love with Arwen and decide to buy her instead but Allison was right. At only 15 hands, Arwen was too small for the tall girl. But she was just right for Shelby, who was one of the shortest girls in her grade. Usually Shelby found her lack of height to be an annoyance, but she would admit that when it came to her riding it had its advantages. Shelby looked just fine on the smaller horses that some of her friends were beginning to outgrow. She could still get away with riding ponies and not look too ridiculous. And for a girl who liked to ride anything and everything, this was a very good thing!

"Hey! It feels so much better today! I think the warm up tip was the key," Chelsea hollered to her as she trotted by.

"Yeah, they are coming along," Allison said as she walked up to Shelby. "They're still having a little trouble down that gymnastic line on the far side."

"Hey, do you think Shelby could get on and go over it so I could watch and see if I'm not doing something," Chelsea trotted over.

"That's a good idea," Allison replied. "Want to hop on?"

Chelsea dismounted and handed Shelby her helmet. Shelby adjusted her stirrups and fit the helmet to her head before climbing aboard.

Settling into the saddle immediately felt like home. She sank into her heels and squeezed the mare forward. Arwen woofed quietly, glad to have her old pal on her back.

Shelby squeezed the mare into a springy trot, half halted, and put the mare in a beautiful frame. She squeezed the fingers on her outside rein and applied just a little calf pressure on her inside leg as she asked the mare to round up underneath her. After a quick warm up, Shelby picked up a canter and held the mare steady as she headed for the outside line. She knew Arwen could get a little strung out if you didn't hold her in a neat little package approaching the first jump.

She figured this was what was eluding Chelsea. She'd had a hard time figuring it out as well. With most of the other school horses, you approached a line and gave them a little leeway with their head. They found their own way over the jumps which made them great for teaching beginners. But Arwen was only 7 and hadn't been jumping that long. She still looked to her rider for confidence and support.

Shelby kept a firm grip on the reins, setting up a wall with her hands and continued to drive the mare forward with her seat. Arwen pricked her ears at the line of three jumps in front of her, but remained steady under the guidance of her rider. After the first fence, Shelby closed both legs around the mare sending her forward and keeping her straight. Sensing her rider's confidence, the mare boldly jumped the second and third fences and cantered a beautiful closing circle. She appeared rather pleased with herself as Shelby pulled her up next to Allison and Chelsea.

"Ya'll are such a good team!" Chelsea acknowledged admiringly. "I think I need to ride her a little more forward. Really send her to the jump."

Allison nodded in agreement. She always preferred for her riders to figure out the answers to their problems on their own. It was one of the reasons she allowed riders to ride outside of their weekly lessons.

"Yep, Arwen gets her confidence from her rider. When you soften your hand and stop riding her forward she feels like you are hesitating. So she hesitates. But when you keep your leg on her and keep driving her, she's very game to go over anything. Socks will be the same way. You can't be a passenger on a horse like this. You must ride to and through the jump. Try again?"

As Chelsea readjusted her stirrups she whispered to Shelby. "Thanks! I'm having so much fun and learning so much. You make riding her look so easy!"

Shelby smiled at her, humbled. She'd been riding since she was eight and was always willing to ride anything she could put a saddle on. She attributed that, and having Allison as a trainer as the reasons she was such a good rider for her age. Each horse had something new to teach. None of them worked the exact same way. You have to find what makes them tick.

Chelsea's next attempt at the gymnastic line was much more successful. She cooled the mare down and walked with Shelby and Allison back to the barn.

Chapter 4

Taylor was stretched out across her bed with her head hanging off, picking at the carpet. The two girls were supposed to be finishing a school project and although they were almost done had decided to take a quick break to talk about horses.

"So Chelsea's parents said they'd buy her a horse instead of a car for her sixteenth birthday?" Taylor asked.

"Yep. She said she can still use the family car if she needs to, but it was a no brainer to take them up on the horse offer."

"Pretty cool! Do you think your folks will ever get you a horse?"

Shelby sighed. She dreamed of owning her own horse but knew that the reality of it was unlikely. Just the cost of the initial horse was expensive, especially one that would be able to be competitive at showing, but then you have to factor in board, farrier and vet bills. It didn't seem very likely to happen.

"Probably not. I know they'd love to try, but horses are expensive. Probably not going to happen any time soon. Maybe if we win the lottery?" she joked.

"I'm just excited to get to show the Rivermont series this year!" Taylor said excitedly.

Allison believed in her riders having a pretty solid seat and leg before she allowed them to show. Therefore, her riders often started showing a little later than many other barns. It paid off as High Lane Farm riders often garnered top honors at the local shows. Taylor had showed last fall in two very small shows but this would be her first experience with a bigger show series.

"I know! I'm ecstatic that we'll be doing the shows together this year. We're going to be unstoppable!"

"The first show is in three weeks! I can't believe it's coming so soon. When do you think I will find out who I'm riding? I hope I get to show Avenue. We are a good match," Taylor stated.

"Allison will tell you soon. We have a group lesson tomorrow. Maybe you could ask her then."

High Lane Farm's lesson program typically placed riders in small groups of three or four depending on age and experience. But at least once a month, several of the groups would join together for a big group lesson. Allison thought it was a great way for the less advanced riders to watch and learn skills from the riders with more experience and gave the more skilled riders the responsibility of helping teach. Plus, it was good practice to ride in a crowded arena with horses of all levels and speeds. Shelby loved these lessons. She enjoyed learning from superior riders and helping those coming along. Taylor was doing crossrails, so they didn't normally lesson together. So it was fun to have group lessons to look forward to riding.

"Is Arwen ready for the 2'6" hunter course?" Taylor asked.

"I think so. We've sure been practicing! She'll get a little more nervous at a show but I think I can keep her steady. Plus, we will do some flat classes first to warm her up."

The Rivermont Series held a monthly show that had a wide variety of classes for all levels of riders. They had flat classes, where the riders performed in a group at a walk, trot and canter. There were also over fences classes. The show offered classes for beginners just ready for their first show all the way up to high level jumping classes. The best part was, the show was only twenty minutes away so High Lane Farm was a regular participant.

"Girls, how's the project coming?" Taylor's mom asked peeking in the door.

"Um, okay," Taylor muttered. "Guess we need to finish it up. These paragraphs aren't going to write themselves."

Shelby scrunched her nose but reached for her notebook and the girls got back to work.

Chapter 5

"Reverse at the posting trot. Watch your spacing. Keep your eyes up. Use soft, guiding hands." Allison hollered from the center of the arena where seven riders were circling around her. "If you are riding a chestnut horse, drop your stirrups and continue at the posting trot."

Three riders groaned in protest, including Taylor. No stirrup work was difficult, but necessary for strengthening leg muscles and seat development. But not too many riders looked forward to it.

Shelby took a second to get prepared, knowing she'd likely be in the next group asked to drop stirrups. Sure enough after several laps, Allison had the remaining riders drop their stirrups. Those riding the chestnuts breathed a sigh of relief as they found their stirrups again.

Arwen rode like a dream and Shelby could feel that all of the extra time in the saddle was paying off for both of them. She felt stronger and more capable as a rider. In return, Arwen was a trusting and willing partner. Shelby felt a twinge of excitement about the upcoming show season and she tried to suppress it. For one thing, the first show was three weeks away and Shelby still felt they had plenty to work on. She also wasn't the type of rider who liked to focus on the ribbon. Sure, she'd love to win, and she'd be lying if she said the thought of blue ribbons didn't excite her. But she and Arwen had come so far together and staying positive and continuing their partnership was what was most important to Shelby. It was a big step. This was Arwen's first show series and Shelby was moving up to the 2'6" course. Shelby really just wanted them to have fun and enjoy the experience. If they brought home some blue ribbons, that would be the icing on the cake.

As the lesson wrapped up, Shelby dismounted and ran up her stirrups. She loosened Arwen's girth and took off her helmet, shaking her hair loose. She and Taylor met at the gate and decided to hand walk their horses in the stable yard to cool them down.

The early March air was chilly so Shelby zipped her jacket. Arwen buried her head in Shelby's chest, eager for some love.

"What a beautiful girl you are! Thank you for trying so hard today." Shelby whispered to her.

The two girls and their horses walked together in silence.

"I asked Allison about the show," Taylor began. "She said she's pretty positive I will be riding Avenue." She patted the pretty chestnut gelding. "We are doing the crossrails classes. I think that's a good starting point, don't you?"

"Perfect. You are already confident over crossrails so it will be a piece of cake even if you get a little nervous."

"Ugh, I'm already nervous! Or maybe that's excitement. Or both! Either way, I've got butterflies in my stomach!"

Shelby laughed with her friend. She knew she would be nervous too, as the show grew closer. But for now she was content to put off

thinking about it and take each ride as it
happened.

Back in the stable, all of the students
bustled around untacking horses, brushing them
down and putting lightweight blankets on for the
night. Some cleaned stalls, while others fed hay
and watered. It was one of the many things
Shelby loved about High Lane Farm. Everyone
participated and was responsible for more than
just riding. And everyone helped each other.

Riders joked and laughed and scratched
their horses as the stable was tidied and parents
arrived. Shelby knew her mom would be few
minutes late as she was picking up Tucker from
karate. Shelby didn't mind though. It gave her a
few minutes to enjoy the quiet as the horses
munched their dinner.

She opened Arwen's stall door and closed it
behind her and greeted the mare with a pat. Then
she sat down in her favorite spot, underneath the
corner feeder, by Arwen's pile of hay. She could
visit with the mare as she happily munched her
dinner , content and secure in her stall. Some
horses didn't care much for stalls but Arwen

didn't mind. On chilly nights she seemed especially appreciative to have a cozy place with deep soft bedding to spend the night.

Arwen rooted around in her hay pile digging out the alfalfa, her favorite. She shoved a pile over toward Shelby as if offering to share and looked perplexed when Shelby burst out laughing. "What a special horse!" she thought, "I'm so glad she's my partner. She rubbed the mare's forehead and daydreamed of jumping big fences until she heard a car in the driveway. She gave the mare a quick pat before locking the stall behind her and heading out into the night.

That evening after dinner, Shelby approached her sister, Sage, about helping her with some homework. Sage had just turned sixteen and was super smart, especially with computers. She was a computer whiz.

"I know I saved my file on this flash drive, " Shelby told Sage as they sat down at the family computer. "It's a two page essay. I really don't want to retype it, but I can't find it anywhere!"

Sage took the mouse and looked around for the file.

"It's not on here," Sage replied. "But hold on, let me look some more. What did you name the file?"

"I dunno. English1, maybe?" Shelby answered weakly.

Sage gave her a withering look.

"Brilliant," she said sarcastically. "Ah ha! Here it is! You saved it on the hard drive. Do I need to show you the difference again?"

"No, no. I got it. I must have been distracted. Thanks for your help. Whew! I'm so glad I don't have to retype it! So I heard Mom and Dad saying that they found a car for you?"

Sage grinned, "Yeah, I'm pumped! Although I think the main reason I'm getting a car is to help with your barn transportation and Tucker's stuff. But that's okay. It's wheels!"

"My friend Chelsea, at the barn is getting a horse instead of a car for her sixteenth birthday. I think that's what I'd want."

Sage puckered her face in protest. "You and those horses!"

It was no secret that Sage was not much of a horse person. She'd been out to the barn a time or two to try to be supportive but she was more worried about getting dirty and seemed a little intimidated by their size. It was hard for Shelby and Sage to find much in common. Sage was super smart and very artistic. She was very talented with photography and graphic design and took all the advanced computer classes at school. Shelby was proud of her sister but it still didn't give them much to talk about.

"You good now?" Sage asked her sister.

Shelby nodded.

"Good. I'm going to get back to my homework. Flash drive next time!" Sage teased bonking her sister on the head with the small disk.

Chapter 6

The phone rang in the darkness. Shelby fumbled for her alarm thinking that was where the sound was coming from. It took her a minute to realize it was her cell phone. She'd been given a cell phone only in case of absolute emergency, so it never rang. Her heart quickened when she saw Allison's name pop up on the screen.

"Hello?" she asked wearily. "Allison?"

"Shelby," a shaken voice on the other end answered. "It's Arwen. There...there's been an accident. I think you should come. Do you think your mom could bring you? It's not good Shelby. I know how much you love her. I'm so sorry." Allison was crying now.

"What? No..." Shelby started to cry, too. "No. What happened? I'll be right there."

She hung up the phone before waiting for an answer. She had to get to the barn. Crying she ran out to the kitchen where her mom was already up starting coffee.

"Shelby? What are you doing up so early? What's wrong, honey?"

"It's Arwen, Mom. Something's happened. An accident. I don't know. Allison called me and told me I better come. She said it's not good, Mom. It's not good."

She was wrapped in her mother's arms sobbing when Sage walked into the kitchen. Shelby's mother took charge.

"Sage, there's an emergency. I need you to get Tucker to the bus stop on time. 7:15, okay? You can get a ride with Lindsay across the street. Shelby, get dressed. I'll pack you something to eat. Give me a minute to get dressed. Go!"

Shelby fumbled around in her dark room pulling on some jeans and a sweatshirt. She blew her nose and stuffed extra tissue in her pocket. Not Arwen, she pleaded. What on earth could have happened?

Shelby stumbled into the kitchen where her brother was pouring a bowl of cereal.

"Hey, Shelby gets to skip school? No fair!" he complained.

Her mother shot him a dirty look. "Yes. Just this once. Now eat up and don't be trouble for Sage."

She herded Shelby out the door and into the car where they drove to the barn in silence.

Shelby hopped out of the car at the barn and ran in with her mother following behind. Allison was standing at Arwen's stall staring into it with her shoulders slumped and her eyes red from crying. She looked to be in a state of shock.

"Hi," she said glumly. "I'm sorry. I didn't think about school or anything. I was just panicked." She sent Shelby's mom an apologetic look.

"No worries. I'm glad you called. This horse is important to Shelby."

"Dr. Benson is on the way. She got stuck in her stall last night. I don't know how it happened," Allison's voice shook. "She must have reared or....something. She got a hoof stuck in between the stall bars. She was lying on her back with her hoof stuck in the stall suspended above her when I got here to feed. I'll bet she's broken a leg. She won't put weight on it. Have a look, but don't go in yet. She's not steady."

Shelby finally dared to peek in at her beloved Arwen. In the dimly lit stall she could make out her beautiful mare. She wasn't putting any weight on her front right leg instead, she had it propped at the toe. The mare was wet with lather and covered in shavings. Blood smeared her legs marring up her bright white socks. It was a gruesome sight. Worst of all, she didn't seem to realize that anyone was there. She faced the back of the stall, head down, sides heaving.

"When is the vet getting here? Shouldn't he hurry?" Shelby panicked.

"He'll be here as soon as he can. At least she is standing, that's good."

Shelby noticed the bars where her leg must have been trapped as they were now bent.

She realized Allison must have been the one to have to deal with freeing the trapped mare by herself. How scary for her! She saw the wood separating Arwen's stall from the next stall, broken and splintered in places where Arwen must have kicked and struggled to try to free herself. Her shredded blanket was thrown in the corner feeder. Shelby wondered how long her poor horse had been hung. She bit her lip to keep from crying.

The big barn opened and Dr. Benson backed his vet truck down the aisle. He got out, said a quick hello and walked over to assess the situation.

After a look, he turned to Allison and said, "Lots of things I am concerned about, obviously. She doesn't appear to have any broken bones in the leg that are extreme anyways. I'm concerned about the elbow. Depending on how long she was hung and how hard she struggled she could have damaged that. The other concern is the cut she sustained on her knee. It's deep and is right there along the joint. If she cut into the joint capsule, it could become infected which is not good."

He paused, reevaluating the mare. He scratched her on the withers. "I don't want to jump to any conclusions right now. She is in shock. She needs some time to settle and then we'll really be able to tell what's hurting. Let's wait until tomorrow, maybe shoot some x-rays and talk about our options. She's going to be in pain today of course, but I don't think it's anything that can be managed."

"So you're saying she has a chance?" Shelby blurted out.

Dr. Benson smiled kindly at her. "I can't make any promises. But we can see what tomorrow brings."

Shelby felt relief wash over her. She'd been prepared to have to say goodbye to Arwen right then and there. She didn't think she'd be able to do it. She realized there was still a long road ahead but she was glad to have a little more time with her special horse. Besides, Arwen is a fighter, Shelby thought.

Allison asked Shelby to hold Arwen's lead rope while she and Dr. Benson discussed all of the care she would need. Tears streamed down Shelby's face as she placed a cheek on Arwen's neck. With her legs shaking she realized just how scared she had been that she might lose the horse. And it was still a possibility, but at least Shelby had a little time to prepare.

"What did you do? Oh Arwen, what happened?" she whispered. Arwen blew her hot breath into Shelby's hand and sighed deeply. The pain medicine the vet had given her was starting to kick in and the mare's breathing was returning to normal.

"Here. I should hold her while we get this leg cleaned up, just in case she gets a little squirrely." Allison said taking the lead rope from Shelby and putting her arm around her. "Go sit for a minute. You look pale."

The enormity of the situation had finally hit Shelby and she felt light headed. She let her mother lead her into the office where she convinced her to eat a granola bar and drink some juice.

When she felt better, Shelby returned to watch the vet bandage the mare.

"She'll need both legs bandaged for support. She's going to have major swelling so this will help it somewhat. Shelby, can you dig through that box there and pick out some wraps for her?"

Shelby dug through the box and selected several rolls of bright pink vet wrap. She felt a little silly as she handed the pink wraps to Dr. Benson. Perhaps she should have chosen the more dignified black or red.

But Dr. Benson winked at her, "Good choice. She's going to need a cheery color to keep her spirits up."

After Arwen was bandaged and resting quietly in her stall and Allison had a bucket of wraps and medicine to use, Dr. Benson headed out with a promise to return the next morning. Allison collapsed on a bench by the tack room. She put her head in her hands and rubbed her forehead.

"Wow, what a morning. This was not what I had planned for the day!" she tried to joke.

Shelby's mom delivered a fresh cup of coffee to her and convinced her to sit while she helped Shelby finish up morning chores.

After all the horses were eating breakfast, Shelby's mom left with the promise to return later with some lunch. Shelby sat outside Arwen's stall and worked on cleaning tack to keep her mind occupied.

Chapter 7

Luckily, the next day was Saturday so Shelby didn't have to worry about skipping school. Shelby's mom had been supportive of missing one day but Shelby knew that was all she was getting.

The barn was quiet early on a Saturday morning, but Shelby knew it would come to life in a short amount of time as students showed up for lessons.

The mare seemed much perkier than she had the day before and Shelby was relieved to see that she didn't appear to be in major pain. She moved slowly to the stall door as Shelby opened it and bent her head checking Shelby's pockets for treats.

"Silly girl. Glad you have your appetite," Shelby whispered.

Allison approached Shelby and gently put an arm around her, "Well, do you want to hear what the vet and I talked about earlier this morning?"

Shelby shrugged and nodded slowly. She did want to know but wasn't prepared for bad news.

Allison continued, "We took some x-rays and didn't see anything glaringly obvious. There are still a lot of things that could be wrong but we decided to take it day by day and see how she is doing. It's going to be a long road to recovery. And Shelby..." Allison paused looking directly at her. "She may never be a riding horse again."

Tears rolled down Shelby's face, both sadness and relief. She had never considered the possibility that the mare might survive only to be incapable of carrying a rider.

"I'm not telling you this to be mean or that I don't think Arwen can recover. I just want you to be prepared, that's all," Allison explained. "We will all do everything we can and I'm going to need your help. We'll give it our best shot and I know Arwen will too, won't you girl?" I will give you a minute for everything to sink in, then come into the office. I could use your help with some things."

Shelby stood in the stall, contemplating everything she'd just heard. A million thoughts raced through her mind. She pet the mare absent mindedly then turned to go as a bewildered Arwen nudged her. Now that she had her pain medicine, the mare felt fine and didn't understand all the fuss.

Shelby latched the door behind her and hurried to the office. Students were starting to arrive and Shelby just wasn't in the mood to see anyone yet. She closed the door to the office and sank into the couch. Her eye landed on the show bill for the Rivermont Show. She realized that with everything going on the show was not important, but she felt disappointed anyway. Everything had unraveled the last two days and Shelby didn't know how to process it.

Allison walked in the office and closed the door. She caught Shelby's eyes lingering on the show bill.

"I know you are disappointed. We will figure something out. You are showing at that show and you are going to be a contender for the year end award, I just know it!"

She sat down at her desk and opened up her planner. She studied it intently and seemed to be working things out in her head. The she continued, "I know he's not Arwen, but Midas is a nice horse and very capable in the 2'6". I think you should plan on showing him, okay?"

Shelby nodded. Midas Touch was a lesson horse that she had very much enjoyed riding before she'd moved up to Arwen. The grey Arabian gelding was a packer and always did his job. He'd be just fine in the 2'6" division although Shelby knew he wouldn't do as well as Arwen would have. Arwen looked the part of a show horse when she was doing her thing. She had pizazz and class. She looked like a winner. Midas was sweet, kind and consistent, but he didn't quite have that extra spark that Arwen brought to the table. Still, Shelby knew she would be grateful to have something to show so last minute and she loved Midas, she really did. The gray horse's smooth canter would surely help her do well in her equitation classes.

"Take the day off if you want, but get back in the saddle soon," Allison urged. "It will help you sort everything out. In the meantime, I could use your help down at the arena moving jumps around."

Shelby groaned, but she grinned at Allison. Moving jumps was not her favorite chore but it would certainly work to take her mind off of everything. And maybe she would see if she could take Midas for a quick trail ride later. She may as well begin practicing on him if they were going to be ready to show. The big day was only two weeks away.

Chapter 8

Monday afternoon, Shelby and Taylor rode the bus to the barn after school. They planned to take a trail ride then finish with some cavaletti work in the ring. Cavalettis were a great exercise for building strength in both horse and rider. Over the weekend Shelby had taken a great ride on Midas and was looking forward to riding him again. And she couldn't wait to see Arwen. Allison had told her today she could take her out in the stable yard to nibble some grass. Shelby knew the mare would be thrilled to be outside.

When they walked into the barn, Chelsea ran up to Shelby and threw her arms around her. "I'm so sorry. I can't even imagine. I was gone this weekend so I just found out the news. Are you doing okay?"

Shelby hugged her back. She was still heartbroken but she was coming to terms with it more each day.

"I'm okay. I'm just glad she's got a chance. It was so scary," she admitted.

Chelsea nodded sympathetically, "If you ever want to talk, I'm here, okay? But right now, I've got saddles to clean." She rolled her eyes jokingly.

Shelby decided to let Arwen out while she had Taylor around to help. Allison had explained to her that stall rest was best for Arwen right now, but she would need a little break to get out and enjoy the sunshine. For now, Shelby would be able to handle the mare but the longer Arwen was cooped up in a stall the more stir crazy she would get. Allison warned her that after a while only Allison may be able to handle her. So Shelby wanted to take advantage of every second while she could. The mare was grateful and tugged around at the end of the lead rope searching for the best blades of grass.

Allison had just come in from teaching a lesson as Shelby was putting Arwen back in her stall.

"Can I get you to put your ride on hold?" she asked Shelby.

"Sure, what's up?"

"I've got an idea for you. I was talking to my friend, Judy, who runs the rescue and she's been doing a lot of auction rescues lately. People dump these poor horses for whatever reason, but many of them are perfectly good riding horses. Anyway, she's got this pony that's a cute jumper that she needs to sell. He would do best if someone like you could ride him, and maybe show him so people could see that he'd be a good kid's pony. Whatcha think?"

"That sounds fun! Where is he?"

"Well, he's at the rescue but I already talked to your mom. If you want to, you and I can go ride him this afternoon. Taylor, too. I figured you'd be okay with it."

"Would I show him?" Shelby asked.

"Hopefully. I guess it depends on how well you get along with him but that would be my hope. I know it's not a long term solution, but it might be fun and it would really help out the rescue. Judy is going to use the profit of these sales to help fund more rescues."

Shelby nodded quickly, "That's awesome! And you know me, I love to ride anything I can. Sounds fun. When do we leave?"

"In just a minute. Let me finish up a few things here. Grab your helmet and Taylor, and meet me in the truck."

Shelby quickly found Taylor and explained the situation. Her friend was more than happy to give up her afternoon ride especially since it meant a chance to go see the equine rescue.

"So what do you know about this pony?" Taylor asked excitedly as the three of them pulled out of the driveway.

"Not much. Apparently he's a really neat jumper and his name is Mittens."

"Cute," Shelby said but inside she groaned. Mittens sounded like a six year old's pony. She hoped she wasn't going to be asked to show some teeny tiny kid's pony and look like a fool. She was short, but even she would look funny on a tiny pony.

They pulled up to the rescue and were greeted by several dogs and an older lady with her hair pulled into a ponytail and a big sun hat on her head.

"This must be the rider I've heard so much about!" she said shaking Shelby's hand. "I'm Judy. It's so nice to meet you. Thanks for helping out."

She led the way into the barn. "Come meet Mittens. He's in the crossties and ready to go."

Shelby was relieved to see a lovely gray pony about 14 hands, standing in the crossties.

"This was a rescue?" Taylor asked, bewildered.

"I'm afraid so. Although you can't tell now that he's gained some weight. He's a Welsh pony, about 14 years old. I had to piece together part of his history. He was quite the children's hunter several years ago. There were stories of him becoming a bit of a bucker, so my guess is that whoever owned him just got rid of him. He bounced around through several owners until he wound up at the auction, scared and skinny. I just had to have him. He's a nice fellow. I had the chiropractor work on him. She said his back was all out of whack so that would be the cause for the bucking. He's as good as new, now. He'll make some kid a nice pony."

Shelby liked Judy instantly. She could tell she took great care of her animals and was loving and kind. She admired the work she did and was glad for the opportunity to help.

"What do you think, Shelby? Want to take him for spin?" Judy asked.

Shelby nodded enthusiastically and they set to tacking him up. They took a few minutes to lunge him before Shelby rode to make sure he was going to behave but he mostly seemed lazy. There was no trace of the former bucker in this pony.

From the moment she swung over his back, Shelby could tell the pony was like a well-oiled machine. He'd obviously received a lot of training at some point in his life.

"What crazy person gave this pony away?" she asked incredulously.

"Greed does powerful things to people. If he was bucking and acting out, he was keeping some rider from winning. So it was probably easier to get rid of him and move on to another horse that could win," Allison explained. "Of course all of this is speculation, but he has obviously been very well trained at some point. He'll be able to be sold for a decent amount of money. It will really help the rescue."

Shelby didn't doubt it. She knew well trained ponies like this were worth their weight in gold and trainers and parents would pay good money to have one. She decided to make it her personal goal to help Judy find the perfect home for Mittens, where he would be loved and appreciated for everything he was.

Allison gave the pair a quick mini lesson with Taylor and Judy cheering for them. The gray pony was perfectly willing and Shelby was amazed at how easily he handled the height of the jumps.

"The 2'6" jump feels like nothing. You'd never know he was only 14 hands," Shelby marveled. "What a talented guy!"

She and Taylor brushed his shiny coat in the crossties after the ride.

"He seems to appreciate all of this attention," Taylor observed. "I guess he's seen the other side of what can happen."

Judy agreed. "That's the funny thing about rescues. They really do seem to appreciate everything you do for them. Some people would disagree, but most rescues really try hard to please the people who show them love. Would you girls like to meet some of the other residents here?"

"Oh, we'd love to!" Taylor exclaimed. "Come on Shelby, let's meet some horses."

The girls got the farm tour meeting most of the other horses. There were a few retirees who would stay at the farm forever, receiving love and care. Judy had a few rescues that were ready to be rehomed, and a few others who were working hard to gain both weight and trust in humans.

"Rescues aren't all dramatic abuse situations," Judy explained about a very affectionate pinto mare. "Some are just cases of people who can no longer afford to properly care for their animals. They love them, but they don't quite realize that they aren't caring for them properly. That's what happened to this sweet girl. Luckily her owner surrendered her to us. We'll get her all fixed up and find her a great new home."

"That sounds so rewarding," Taylor said.

"It is. It can be. Of course, we see lots of sad things, too. But we are just glad to be able to do what we can and help some of these horses find people who can care for them."

"I'd be glad to help ride any of them that you need to help rehome," Shelby offered.

"And I can help groom. I'm really good at getting horses looking their best," Taylor added.

"Oh, girls! That would be wonderful! I've got several of these horses ready to be sold but selling isn't my forte. Allison offered to help but she is so busy, of course. If you girls would help that would just be perfect. We'd have a good time, too," Judy winked at them.

"I've got some ideas for selling. Let me do some research," Shelby said. "When do you want me to ride Mittens again?"

"You just come on out whenever. I'm usually here. You'll need to practice if you're going to show him. So exciting!"

Shelby and Taylor made plans to come back after school the next day. Shelby started scheming ways to help the rescue find great homes for the horses.

Chapter 9

Later that night, Shelby cornered Sage in her room.

"Hey, I need your help!"

"Okay," Sage eyed her wearily. "What's with the excitement?

"It's a project that we can work on together that I think we will both enjoy. Plus, it's for a great cause."

Shelby told her about the rescue and how Judy had several horses that she needed help to advertise and sell.

"You're so good at editing videos and taking pictures. I just know that with your help we'd be able to do some great marketing for these horses. And you can help me list them all online and find them amazing homes. These poor horses deserve it. Please, Sage!" she pleaded.

Sage pondered it. "I suppose I always need the extra practice with video editing. And it would probably look great on a college application to help with an equine rescue. Okay! What do we need to do to get going?"

Shelby shrieked and hugged her sister. "Oh, yay! I'm so excited. This will be great. First we'll need to get the horses all cleaned up. Taylor and I will do that. Then I will need you to help me get pictures and videos. Maybe this weekend? I don't know. I'll have to double check with the owner, Judy, but she will be so glad to have the help."

The next day at school, Shelby filled Taylor in on her plan. Taylor readily agreed to help in whatever way she could. She volunteered to do research on the best online sites to list horses for sale as well as be in charge of making sure all the horses looked their best.

"I can make a chart with each horse and everything we need to do", she explained to Shelby. "That will be the most effective use of our time and nothing will get left out."

Taylor was very organized and methodical and Shelby knew it would come in very handy.

That afternoon at the rescue, Shelby and Taylor offered their ideas and services to Judy, who was overwhelmed with enthusiasm.

"Girls, this would mean so much to the rescue to help these horses find loving homes. I am just not savvy with the computer at all, so if you wanted to step in and help organize all that it would be much appreciated. We rescued so many horses this winter that we are really at max capacity. We desperately need to find homes for some of these guys so we can bring in others that need our help.

"Oh we aren't just going to find them homes," Taylor stated, "We are going to find them the best homes possible. We will have these horses all clipped and groomed and looking so good that people will be lining up at the door!"

Judy laughed. "Well, I appreciate your optimism and your help. But also don't forget that you've got a show coming up. I'd hate for

Allison to be upset with me because you aren't prepared enough."

"Oh, no. Don't worry, we will get in plenty of practice. Plus, I have to ride Mittens here," Shelby put in.

"And High Lane Farm is practically around the corner. So if we don't have too much homework, we can go to both barns," Taylor added.

"Well, if you say so. Let's get to work," Judy replied.

Judy introduced the girls to the first four horses that she was hoping to sell, including Mittens. They talked about each horse's history, what it would be best suited for and a fair asking price. Taylor took detailed notes and true to form, had charts and a general plan outlined by the end of the visit.

Depending on what discipline the horse was best suited for would determine the type of grooming done such as how much clipping, whether or not to pull the mane, as well as what type of pictures and videos would best market each horse.

There was an Appaloosa mare named Sally who was about fourteen years old. She had come to the rescue underweight and with an injured hoof. Although the injury had been treated and was healed, the mare was best suited for light riding. She was brave and willing though and Judy thought she would make an ideal partner for someone who wanted to trail ride lightly once or twice a week.

The next horse was a spirited Thoroughbred named Capone. The four year old gelding had come from the auction and was sound but untrained. He was very handsome and athletic and would make a perfect partner for an advanced rider who was looking for a project.

The third horse was a darling pony who stood not even twelve hands. Mischief was in his mid-teens and had become easily attached to the other horses in his pasture. He was only suitable to be ridden by very small children and would be a great pet or companion to someone with a lonely horse.

Mittens, was of course the fourth horse that needed a home, and Shelby was very excited to get to play such a large role in rehoming the special pony. After their stellar ride the day before, Shelby just knew he would make some kid very happy.

After discussing all of the details, Judy made the girls promise again that they wouldn't fall behind on their schoolwork or riding practice. When she seemed satisfied that they could keep up with all of it, she agreed to let them spend the next several days getting the horses ready for photos and videos.

Chapter 10

Back at High Lane Farm later in the week, Shelby bustled around gathering things that she needed to take to the rescue. Allison had agreed to give Shelby a lesson on Mittens as well as help with clipping Capone, who could be a handful. Taylor was in the middle of a riding lesson and the girls would leave as soon as she was done.

Shelby took a moment to steal some time with Arwen. She felt guilty for being so busy with Mittens and the rescue, but really there was not much she could do for Arwen right now. Except for a few minutes of hand walking and grazing, Arwen was on stall rest. The vet was pleased with the progress being made with her leg wounds but was still waiting to evaluate the final outcome. Shelby visited almost every day and brought treats and usually gave her a quick grooming. The mare was getting bored, but was still as sweet and affectionate as ever.

Shelby sat in Arwen's stall and observed the chart Taylor had made. The girls had the next day off of school for parent- teacher conferences, and Sage had volunteered to drive them to the rescue and begin taking photos and videos. Then the girls would have all weekend to edit and get their sales pages up online.

"You ready?" Allison peeked in the stall. "Taylor's done, so we've got to go now so I can get back for my last lesson tonight."

"I'm ready." Shelby stood and shut the door behind her giving Arwen a final pat.

Mittens pulled at the reins enthusiastically. Shelby had warmed the pony up with a series of figure eights and a few cavalettis and now the pony seemed to know it was time to jump.

"Okay, okay, let's get to it!" Allison laughed as Mittens snorted at her.

The rescue only had two sets of jumps so Allison had gotten creative with some hay bales and logs. She quickly told Shelby the first course and stepped back to be out of the way.

Shelby sent the pony forward into a smart trot and used his energy to establish a great pace to the first jump. Mittens soared over the first two jumps. Shelby slowed him to a trot to change his lead as she sent him on to the next jump.

"Wait, wait. Let's try that again. I would just about guarantee this pony has flying lead changes. Let's try again and work on that. Come over here for a second," Allison said.

Shelby trotted over and Allison showed her a few techniques to get the pony to swap his leads automatically.

"He may be a little rusty so be very definite with what you are asking. Or better yet, let's try an exercise to get him warmed up."

Allison moved a cavaletti to the center of the ring and showed Shelby the figure eight pattern she wanted her to ride. The cavaletti pole was in the center of the eight and was meant to encourage the pony to change his lead automatically when he crossed it.

Shelby started off on the left lead for the first half of the figure eight. As she approached the pole, Shelby shifted her weight in the saddle and moved her left leg behind the girth as Allison had instructed. Sure enough, as Mittens went over the pole he executed a beautiful flying lead change.

"Whoo hoo! That was good! At least, I think so," Taylor cheered. "It looked right to me."

Shelby smiled as she continued the exercise, this time approaching the pole from the other side of the figure eight on the right lead. Again, Mittens performed a flawless flying lead change.

"Good. Okay, now that he is remembering everything and you guys are in tune, let's try that course again. You'll need to be aware of the lead he lands on after that second jump and adjust it if you need to do so," Allison instructed.

This time Shelby and Mittens nailed the course, performing two flying lead changes when necessary.

"Wow! It is so fun to ride such a well-trained pony!" Shelby praised.

"He is very nice," Allison agreed. "I can't believe he went through the auction!" Allison shook her head in disbelief. "Alright, let's try another course."

Allison put the pair through several challenging courses giving tips and pointers when necessary. When she felt like they had reached a good stopping point, she left Shelby to cool off Mittens and went with Taylor to get started clipping Capone.

Capone stood in the crossties like a gentleman while Taylor pulled his mane. Allison had just finished clipping the horse and was now standing back observing him.

"He is so very handsome," she mused. "I've got some people I can call. He should be easy to find a home for. I kinda wish I had more time for a project."

"Oh, you should!" Taylor exclaimed. "He'd be exciting to have at the farm!"

"Ha, ha! The last thing I need right now is another horse," Allison retorted. "But I know we can find this guy a special home."

Just then Judy walked into the barn looking troubled.

"What's wrong?" Allison asked.

"I just received a call about two horses that need to be rescued. They are coming tomorrow. It sounds like they aren't in great shape." She smiled at the girls. "It's a good thing you girls are here to help me get some horses rehomed. I'm running out of room!"

"What do you know about the two coming tomorrow?" Allison questioned.

"Not much. There is a ten year old gelding and an older horse. I think the older horse is in pretty bad shape. It sounds like they are both thin and haven't had hoof care in quite a while. I don't know anything about their temperaments. Guess we'll find out tomorrow."

Chapter 11

The following morning, Sage, Shelby, and Taylor headed out to the rescue to begin taking photos and videos of the sale horses. Shelby and Taylor had spent a good deal of time over the last few days getting the horses looking their best. Shelby was anxious to get the sales ads put together.

They decided to start with Mischief, the ornery pony. Sage scouted for the best place for photos while Taylor and Shelby brushed the pony until he was shining.

"There's a great spot up near the house where there are some flower bushes. Do you think we could go up there?" Sage asked walking back into the barn.

Shelby shrugged, "I don't see why not. Judy will probably say to do whatever we need to do to get some pretty pictures."

Sage was a talented photographer and quickly captured the personality of the pony with her camera. They decided to also get a short video of him trotting around the arena. They had just finished up with Mischief when Judy pulled in the driveway towing the rescue's two- horse trailer behind her truck.

"This must be the new horses," Taylor speculated. "Poor things. I'm anxious to meet them."

The girls headed over to the trailer to offer their assistance. Judy greeted them as she got out of the truck.

"Morning, girls. I'm afraid we've got some sad cases here. They'll be doing much better now that they'll have some good food to eat. Can you help me get them unloaded and settled in their stalls?"

The girls readily agreed and stood back so Judy could open the trailer door.

Shelby shook her head in disbelief and heard Taylor gasp beside her as the first horse was unloaded.

"This is Roman. He's a twenty-three year old quarter horse," Judy reported.

Shelby could count every one of the poor chestnut gelding's ribs and his haunches stuck out like hangers. His feet were overgrown and had chips and cracks in them. His coat was patchy and dull, and he obviously hadn't been groomed in a very long time. His head hung low to the ground and his eyes were dull. Shelby's eyes immediately filled with tears. She looked to her right, where her sister Sage was standing wearing a very troubled expression. The chestnut gelding looked pitiful.

A loud bang from inside the trailer snapped them all back to reality. Taylor grabbed the lead rope of Roman and led him a safe distance from the trailer so his traveling companion could be unloaded.

There was a lot of stomping and banging as Judy worked to back the nervous horse off the trailer. Finally, he appeared, backing onto the solid ground and whinnying loudly to announce his arrival.

Even in his skinny, dirty state Shelby could tell that he was magnificent. His coat was a dark bay, almost black, and he had two even socks on his front legs. His face was dainty and petite and appeared to be that of an Arabian. He had a large white star evenly centered between his two dark eyes.

"Meet Gatsby," Judy simply said.

The horse eyed them suspiciously then began pulling on the lead rope Judy was holding. He pulled straight over to where Shelby was standing and stopped. He took a moment to sniff her shirt and her hair carefully and when he was satisfied he let out a bored sigh and sneezed horse slobber on her shirt.

Shelby cracked up. "How do you do, Sir?" she giggled. "We really must work on your manners!"

Shelby looked at Judy and said, "He is fantastic. How did he end up like this?"

Although Gatsby was not nearly in as bad of shape as his pasture buddy, Roman, he was still quite skinny. His coat was dull and his mane hung down his shoulder in several large knots. Mud caked his legs and his feet were well overdue for a trim. He appeared to have one shoe on a front hoof that was quite a bit too small and very loose. The other front shoe was nowhere to be seen.

"He is quite the handsome fellow," Judy agreed. "A purebred Arabian, too. I've got the papers in the truck. He and his buddy, Roman, have been living in a sorry excuse for a pasture. They had no shelter and the fencing was barely holding them. The water trough was dirty and disgusting. There was a little bit of a round bale of hay, but it was very poor quality. Several neighbors finally took pity on these poor guys and called us to intervene."

She shook her head sadly as she continued, "Roman is in pretty bad shape and will likely need some dental work to help him be able to gain weight. This guy here is apparently trained under saddle and everything. The owner died and his kids inherited the horses and didn't know how to care for them properly. I think they were happy to be rid of them."

While Judy was talking Shelby had taken Gatsby's lead rope and was allowing him to look around. His ears and eyes took in all of the new sights and sounds of his new environment. He whinnied several times to horses in nearby fields. His eyes sparkled as if he seemed to realize that he had been rescued and everything was going to be okay.

"Let's get them settled in their stalls with some fresh hay and water. Dr. Benson will be out on Monday to give them a good check-up, but in the meantime we will make them comfortable," Judy said.

Taylor and Shelby led the two horses into the stalls that had been prepared. Roman settled in quickly, turning once and settling in front of his pile of hay. Gatsby eagerly sniffed every corner of his new stall. When he was satisfied, he dropped down on his belly for an enthusiastic roll in the shavings. When he stood he had fresh shavings clinging all over his body and stuck in his mane and tail.

"He looks like a porcupine!" Sage exclaimed, laughing.

Gatsby snorted at her then took a long drink of clean water before digging into his flake of hay.

"Well, he looks content," Judy observed.

"I think I'm in love!" Shelby whispered to Taylor.

Taylor nodded in agreement with her friend, "He's a pretty boy."

"Well, you girls will just have to shower him with your love and affection," Judy interjected, overhearing the girls' conversation. "The most important medicine for a rescue is love."

"Oh, you can count on us!" Taylor promised.

"These two love anything with four legs and a tail," Sage teased, but Shelby could see that witnessing these two horses had somehow softened her. Shelby didn't think Sage would become a horse girl, but maybe now her sister would at least kind of understand what horses meant to her.

Shelby smiled at Sage, "Guess we should get back to it, huh? Who should we photograph next?"

The girls spent the whole rest of the day working on photos and videos. Allison came out to help get some good video footage of Capone. She promised that as soon as a video was ready she would send it to several friends who might be looking for a horse with his talent.

The last horse they did was Sally, the sweet Appaloosa. Sage got some great video of Taylor riding the mare over a series of trail obstacles in the arena. Shelby knew any prospective buyer would be impressed with the mare's calm, willing demeanor.

"**W**ell, that's a wrap!" Sage joked as they put the last horse away and began to pick up their stuff in the barn. "I can work on editing tonight and tomorrow and you guys should be able to get the ads up soon. In the meantime, I'm starving! Let's go get some food!"

Shelby snuck away while Taylor and Sage discussed what type of pizza they wanted to order when they got back to the house. She wanted to take a quiet moment to check on Gatsby by herself. All day long, the friendly gelding had been on her mind. She was eager to see him again to see if he was indeed as beautiful and personable as she remembered from their first encounter.

Shelby spoke softly as she unlatched the stall door being careful not to startle the horse. Being as they really had no background information on the horse, Shelby knew he could be unpredictable. But Gatsby just acted like a giant pet. He walked over to her, sniffing her hands for any possible treats. Although he was disappointed with her lack of snacks, he put his muzzle to her cheek and blew softly as if to give her kisses. Shelby slowly reached a hand up to stroke the star on his forehead. Gatsby relaxed and leaned into her touch.

Shelby said goodbye to the horse with a promise to return soon. She was dying to begin a good brushing and detangle that mane, but she knew Taylor and Sage were waiting for her. Before heading back to meet the other girls, Shelby checked on Roman. Even though she didn't feel quite the same affection for him as she did for Gatsby, the old horse was sweet and she didn't want him to feel left out. She was happy to see that Roman's ears were perked up and there was a light in his eyes that she hadn't seen earlier. In just the few hours that he'd been at the rescue, Roman had found hope.

Chapter 12

The next day the rain came down in buckets. Allison called all of her students to cancel lessons with the promise of make-up lessons later in the week. The first show was only one week away and everyone had little things they wanted to work on. Since riding was out of the question, Shelby begged for a ride to the rescue from her dad. She was excited to mess with the new horses.

"I'm running some errands and will pick you up in about an hour," Shelby's dad said as he dropped her at the barn.

"An hour. Got it, see ya then!" Shelby returned closing the car door quickly and running through the rain, dodging rain drops and puddles. The older barn door stuck and Shelby had to use all of her strength to get the door to budge. Finally, it creaked open and Shelby managed to escape the soaking rain.

Once inside the barn, Shelby took a minute to remove her now drenched coat and shove the carrots she had brought into her back pocket. Despite the rain, it was a rather warm spring day and Shelby wouldn't need her coat in the barn. She shook the water out of her hair and pulled it into a sloppy pony tail.

Taylor had been after her all week to meet up and go to the mall to shop for summer clothes. Usually her best friend didn't care what she looked like, but lately she had been showing a little interest in clothes and fashion. Shelby was totally perplexed by this as she was happiest in jeans or riding pants and a t-shirt. Still, she couldn't fault her friend for trying and so she had reluctantly agreed to go shopping. She figured if she played her cards right she could get Taylor to pick out a few things that would look good on her as Shelby had no idea where to start.

A barn cat darted out into the aisle and Shelby watched him bat around a small bundle of bailing twine. She reached down to pet the cat and quickly swiped the twine. She undid part of the string making a simple cat toy and dangled it in front of the kitty. He batted and pawed the string until he got bored and purred against Shelby's leg before disappearing into the tack room.

Shelby loved having the barn all to herself. The rain drummed on the tin roof lightly. The barn was all closed up and warm from the horses all quietly munching their hay. A radio played softly in the background. Shelby sighed contently as she went into the tack room to put together some brushes to begin work on Gatsby.

The horse nickered eagerly to Shelby as she rolled his stall door open. He had been neglected for sure, but it didn't appear as though anyone had mistreated him. He obviously enjoyed people.

Shelby carefully slipped a halter over the horse's head. She wasn't sure if he knew how to crosstie yet, and it could be dangerous to tie a horse that didn't know how to stand quietly, so Shelby just draped the lead rope through the stall bars. She talked quietly to Gatsby and began to curry him. Using a small circular motion, she used the curry comb to loosen dirt and hair. Then she used a brush to get rid of all the dirt and smooth the hair into place. The horse looked shinier already.

After his body had been brushed, Shelby got to work tackling his mane. She used a dab of detangler and smoothed it into the knots. Using her fingers, she managed to untangle most of them. She used a brush to comb out the rest. She did the same with his tail, removing several burrs and old twigs leaving it silky and smooth.

Shelby stood back to admire her work. Gatsby was a beauty and so very sweet. She could see that with proper feeding and some regular grooming he would turn back into the star he used to be. Shelby felt a pang of sadness as she thought about the fact that eventually Gatsby would get all better and would need to find a new home. Whoever ended up with the sweet horse would be very lucky.

Shelby heard the barn door open and looked out the stall to see Judy approaching.

"Hi there!" she greeted Shelby stepping into the stall to admire her work. "You've been busy. He looks incredible! "

"He does, doesn't he?" Shelby murmured stroking Gatsby's neck. "He'll be back to normal in no time at all."

"Well, it might take longer than you think. He still has a long way to go. His feet are in bad shape. It will take several farrier visits before his feet will be free of all of the chips and cracks. And all horses gain weight at different speeds. Some take longer than others. At any rate, he's not going anywhere for a while. And before he can be matched with his new owner, he will need to be evaluated under saddle. I like to make sure I am as aware as I can be of any problems a horse may have before I sell them to a new owner."

"How do you do that?" Shelby inquired.

"We will start with the vet doing an exam to make sure he is healthy and doesn't have any lameness issues. If there are any problems we will see about the necessary treatment. After he has been approved to start some light work, we'll begin some muscle building. I like to start them on the lunge line and then move to ground driving."

"Cavalettis are a great way to add muscle to a horse, and so is conditioning on hills. I used to take Arwen on long trail walks up and down hills. It was hard work...well, hard for me, but it was peaceful and we both enjoyed it," Shelby put in.

"Right! So after the horse is strong enough to carry a saddle and rider we move slowly to restart the horse under saddle. Some horses have already been ridden and they progress quickly, but some of them have had bad experiences and we have to work hard to regain their trust. We want to show them that riding is fun!"

"Gatsby doesn't really seem like he's been abused," Shelby observed. "But I guess you can't really tell until he's under saddle."

"That's true. Both he and Roman are terribly skinny, but neither appears afraid. They are both friendly and sweet. However, sometimes horses have had terrible experiences that they only associate with riding. So they are only scared under saddle. I'm hopeful that we can rehab them, get them under saddle and find them great homes."

"The new owner will be very lucky," Shelby said wistfully.

Judy smiled and nodded. "You could help me get him ready to start under saddle," Judy offered. "He seems very comfortable with you."

Shelby nodded enthusiastically, "I would love that. I'll do whatever you need. With Arwen on stall rest it would be fun to have a project."

"Let's have the vet check him over, but once we get the ok from the vet, perhaps you could start lunging him? Maybe take him on walks around the farm? I will check with Dr. Benson as to how to proceed and let you know, okay? I've got to run back to the house now. You enjoy yourself and be careful!"

Shelby said goodbye then turned to Gatsby and whispered excitedly, "Did you hear that, boy? You and I are going to be partners for a while! We're going to be a great team!"

Chapter 13

"Here, try this on," Taylor said handing Shelby a button up shirt in a flowered print. Shelby scrunched her nose in protest.

"No flowers?" Taylor teased. "Polka dots?"

She handed her a shirt that was blue with white polka dots on it. Somehow it seemed more her style than the flowers so Shelby took it.

"What about some new skirts?" Taylor asked.

"What about some new riding pants?" Shelby answered hopefully. "That sounds more fun to me."

Taylor laughed, "I know, I know. You hate shopping! But I've got to get some new clothes for the summer. I've outgrown everything and all my pants are too short. I've got nothing to wear!"

It was true. Taylor had recently had a growth spurt and now stood four inches taller than Shelby. She was tall and thin, like a dancer and she often joked that she would love to be a dancer, if only she could dance!

Shelby took pity on her friend. "Skirts it is. You lead the way!"

"Yay! Thanks, you're the best. I promise, we'll be quick and then we can get burgers and fries before my mom picks us up!"

"Yum! I'm hungry. What do you think of those?" Shelby asked pointing to a pair of mint green shorts. "They've got pink and yellow, too."

"Cute! I like the pink for me, but definitely the green for you," Taylor replied.

Shelby had long, dark red hair that sometimes made finding clothes difficult. She'd learned rather quickly that she didn't think she looked good in red. And she didn't care much for pink either, but she did like blues and greens. And her mom always said wearing blues and greens brought out the colors in her eyes.

"Okay, hand me a pair in my size," Shelby returned. "And find a shirt that matches. No flowers!"

The girls picked through the racks laughing at some styles that seemed too girly and frilly for them. Taylor found several shirts and a few pairs of shorts for Shelby to try on and quite a few outfits for herself as well. They were just about to head to the dressing room when Taylor stopped.

"Isn't that Corinna Marsh?" she asked quietly.

"Where?" Shelby asked ducking behind the clothing rack.

She looked around. Sure enough, Corinna Marsh and her mother were browsing through some dresses. Shelby groaned. Corinna often showed on the same circuit as the girls. She always had the best of everything- the nicest horse, an expensive saddle, and the latest trends in riding clothes. Worst of all, she didn't seem to care about horses at all. Her mother took care of getting her horse groomed, bathed and saddled at the shows. Corinna just got on and rode.

"We should go say hello," Taylor told her.

"Do we have to?" Shelby muttered.

"Yes. Be nice. I'm sure we will see them next week anyways. Maybe we can find out what horse Corinna is bringing."

Corinna had been known to start the show season with a fancy new mount always a step up from the horse she'd had the year before.

"Okay, but I'm not staying long. All this shopping has me famished."

"You and your stomach! Come on!" Taylor dragged Shelby across the store.

"Hello, Corinna, Mrs. Marsh," she said politely.

"Oh, look! Hello, girls! How are you doing? Are you getting excited about the show next weekend? I assume High Lane Farm will be there?" Mrs. Marsh questioned.

"We will. We are taking quite a few riders and horses," Shelby responded. " What about you? Will you guys be going?"

"Oh, we sure will!" Mrs. Marsh said excitedly. "Corinna has a new horse!"

"He's a thoroughbred. He has Secretariat and Native Dancer in his bloodlines," Corinna said smugly.

Shelby knew this was meant to impress her although plenty of thoroughbreds these days had famous race horses somewhere in their history. Still she tried to act impressed.

"Nice. What does he look like?" Taylor asked.

"He's a chestnut. About 15.2 hands," Corinna responded looking bored. She went back to flipping through the dresses on the rack in front of her.

"He's lovely," Mrs. Marsh continued, clearly thrilled with their new gelding. "He's from a well-known farm down in Florida. He's had extensive training. We think it should be a good year!"

"What division are you showing?" Shelby asked Corinna.

Corinna started to answer but Mrs. Marsh interrupted, "Well, the horse has shown 3'6" but I believe we will start with the 2'6" hunter division.

He and Corinna are just getting to know each other so there is no need to rush."

Shelby figured this meant one of two things. Either Corinna was over-horsed and was having trouble getting the gelding around a course or they wanted to be sure they had the best advantage of taking home the most blue ribbons. Mrs. Marsh loved to win. Shelby decided not to let it bug her either way. Mittens was a nice pony whether he won or not, and Shelby just wanted to do her best to find him a great home. If Corinna was going to be riding her fancy new horse in the 2'6" hunter division too, Shelby would just be sure to give them a run for their money!

After a little more small talk and a promise to see them the following weekend, the girls said their goodbyes and parted ways with the Marshes. They headed to the dressing room to try on clothes and make their final selections. Both Shelby and Taylor's mothers had trusted them to do their own shopping this time and had given them a little money to spend. Shelby would have much rather spent the money on something horse related, but she did have to admit that some of the shirts she picked out were cute and the mint green shorts were super comfortable.

After making their purchases, the girls headed to the food court to grab some burgers before Taylor's mom picked them up.

"Corinna's mom is kind of....Intense," Taylor mused after ordering her cheeseburger and tater tots. "I think it would be exhausting to have a mother like that."

"She's been that way as long as I've known her. Very into winning," Shelby said.

"She didn't even ask what divisions we would be riding or what horses we were bringing!" Taylor pointed out.

"She doesn't really care," Shelby explained. "It's all about Corinna. I honestly think that she thinks that no one will be able to beat that fancy new horse of theirs."

Taylor grinned as Shelby continued, "But that little gray pony and I plan to give it our best shot! We've been working really hard and he's a talented pony. Maybe, just maybe, we'll surprise them!"

Chapter 14

The next afternoon Sage finally finished up all of the photos and videos and sat down with Shelby to help her get them online. Shelby and Taylor had already sat down with Judy and figured out what each horse's ad should say so it would just be adding in all of the necessary information and uploading the photos and videos.

They sat down at the computer and Sage showed Shelby some of her favorite photos.

"Look at this one. This pony is so cute. Look at his expression. And he even has his ears perked up!"

Sage was referring to a photo of Mischief she had taken. The pony had just seen a cat walk by and was very curious about what the cat was doing. In the photo his neck was arched and his ears were perked. He looked like quite a handsome pony!

"If this doesn't sell him, nothing will!" Shelby proclaimed.

"And I love this one of you and Mittens," Sage mentioned pointing to a fantastic photo of the pair jumping over an oxer. The photo had captured a moment where horse and rider were in perfect harmony. Mittens looked the part of a hunter pony with his knees evenly tucked to his chin. Shelby was executing perfect equitation and the pair looked unstoppable.

"Oh!" Shelby gasped. "Wow, that's really good! You're GOOD at this, Sage."

Sage blushed. "It was kinda fun. And it was harder than I expected to get the perfect shots. I think the challenge added to the fun of it."

Shelby sat back admiring the photo of herself and Mittens. "Do you think we could get this one blown up and printed? I'd love to frame it and hang it in my room."

"Sure. We've even been learning at school on how to do our own developing. I can ask my teacher. But even if that doesn't work, we can get it enlarged just about anywhere."

"Awesome! Thanks!" Shelby said.

The girls went through and picked out the top pictures of each horse to use in the ads. Allison and Judy had both told them that people looking for a horse were very interested in seeing lots of photos. Most people also liked to see a video too, if possible, to make sure the horse was what they were expecting. Some people were willing to travel several hours to see a horse they were interested in purchasing. It was best for them to know as much as possible about the horse before making the trip.

Shelby listed each of the horses on several of the most popular horse selling websites. It took several hours, but she finally had all the correct information, photos and video of each horse successfully listed online. She could see how Judy just didn't have time for this! It was quite a feeling of accomplishment and she decided to call Taylor so she could pull the ads up on her computer and admire them, too.

"Hey! I finally finished the ads," Shelby said when Taylor finally got on the phone.

"Cool! Did you use all the websites I recommended? Were they easy to use?"

"Yes and yes. I got them up on all of the sites you gave me. It was pretty self- explanatory and got easier as I went along. I'm glad it's over though. Selling horses is hard work!"

"Well, it's not really over. Judy said that it's also time consuming getting all of the emails and questions that people will have about the horses. Lots of people will take the time to email, but you don't know if they are really serious about the horse."

"I know. Luckily, Judy will be answering most of those emails, because she knows the horses and their history best. I did tell her that one of us would be available if she needs help showing the horses to anybody. That might be fun," Shelby told her.

"Yeah, it would be. Let me know if you need help. Are you going to be at the barn tomorrow?"

"Yeah, I'll be there for the lesson. Allison wants me to ride with the group to practice before the show. I don't know who I'll ride since Mittens is at the rescue, but Allison wanted me to join the equitation lesson. You know what that means, right?"

"Lots of no stirrup work!" Taylor groaned. "Oh, well. At least my legs will have a few days to recover before the show."

The girls hung up to finish homework and prepare for school the next day. Shelby thought about everything she wanted to get in before the show. She was heading to the barn right after school. The lesson wouldn't start for a few hours, but she wanted to take some time to pamper and brush Arwen. She hadn't seen the mare all weekend and she felt guilty about it. She also hoped to talk to Judy soon to find out how Dr. Benson's check with Gatsby and Roman had gone. She needed to get in a few rides on Mittens, plus clean all of her equipment and make sure her show clothes were in tip top shape.

Shelby hoped her teachers would take it easy on her this week with tests and homework. She knew that the family rule was she could only ride and show if she was keeping her grades up and this week she had enough to worry about!

Shelby took the bus from school to the barn. She'd worked all through her study hall and most of the bus ride and had all of her homework just about done. She had a science quiz tomorrow that she still needed to read her notes on, but it should be pretty easy. Plus she was really good in science.

She walked into the barn just as Allison was coming out of her office.

"Just the girl I needed to see! I'm glad you're here early. I've got some good news. Judy called. She had some time this afternoon and thought it might be nice for you to practice with Mittens in a lesson. She's trailering him over in a little bit."

"Really? That's awesome! And it's so nice of her. I'm glad I'll get to ride him. I think the extra practice will do us good. When will she be here? I was hoping to groom Arwen."

"You've got about thirty minutes. Arwen would love some attention. She's been a little bored lately."

"How's her leg doing?" Shelby asked cautiously.

"Pretty good. Dr. Benson is very pleased with the progress her wound is making. As soon as it's not muddy and slippery anymore he's approved for her to start being turned out!"

"That's great! I'm sure she is ready."

"Yeah, it'll be good for her to blow off some steam and act like a normal horse again. As long as she doesn't run around like an idiot, he said she should be able to stay out all day. I'll be glad to not have to clean her nasty stall several times a day!"

Shelby laughed. Arwen was never known for being a tidy stall keeper, but she'd gotten even worse since she'd been inside on stall rest.

"Well, keep an eye out for Judy and Mittens and don't be late for the lesson," Allison requested as she walked to a stall to turn a horse outside.

Shelby headed down the aisle to greet Arwen and feed her some well-deserved treats.

She snuck into her stall delighted with the greeting Arwen gave her, all horse kisses and nuzzles. She whispered all of her latest secrets to the mare, her experience with Gatsby, stories of jumping Mittens and their encounter with the Marshes. Arwen listened earnestly, glad to have some attention from her beloved human.

After a while, Shelby heard a trailer pulling up so she kissed the mare goodbye and ran off to the front of the stable.

Judy waved hello as she backed the trailer into a good spot to unload Mittens. She greeted Shelby warmly as she unloaded the pony and handed Shelby the lead rope.

"Thanks so much for bringing him over here!" Shelby said. "I really think a lesson before the show will be just what we need."

"Of course! It's the least I could do. I'm the one that should be thanking you. Those ads look spectacular! Please tell Sage that she is an incredibly talented photographer. And thanks to you guys we've already gotten several interested phone calls and emails. In fact, I'm pretty sure we've got Mischief sold!"

"Really? Already?" Shelby asked excitedly.

"Yes, a mother called me about the possibility of him for her son. They are an experienced horse family with two other horses. Her son is seven and while he loves horses, he isn't very comfortable riding. He would love a horse to groom, teach some tricks and just love on. His mom thought Mischief would be perfect because of his size. They are coming out tomorrow afternoon to meet him. It sounds like they are excited about him."

"That's great! Mischief deserves a kid who loves him."

"He does. And I have several friends who know this family and said they take super care of their horses. It sounds like he'd have a great home."

"Let me know how it goes! So, has Dr. Benson been out to see Gatsby and Roman yet?" Shelby hinted.

"He sure has. He came out earlier this morning. He gave both horses a full examination and didn't find anything too concerning. He dewormed them both and said they both have mild thrush. He went ahead and floated both of their teeth, although Roman's were in much worse condition. Hopefully that will help them start gaining weight."

Shelby thought there was a pretty good chance that it would. Because of the nature of the way a horse chewed its' food, they often wore their teeth down at different levels. Eventually this could cause sharp points in the mouth that if left untreated could cause the horse pain and force it to eat on one side of the mouth which meant it might not really digest its' food properly. A vet or equine dentist could perform a procedure called floating the teeth, which was basically filing down the sharp points.

"I'll bet they will both feel better soon," Shelby nodded optimistically.

"And we talked about the possibility of starting Gatsby with some light work. Dr. Benson thought it would be a good idea as long as he is started slowly. He thought some light lunging at a walk and trot, as well as some good hand walks around the property would be really good for him. The farrier is coming out tomorrow to trim his feet and pull that shoe. Maybe Thursday you could come work with him?"

"Yes!" Shelby cried, "I would love to work with him. I will be there."

"Perfect. I know he would enjoy some attention from you. He seems very partial to your company. Now don't let me keep you. I know you've got a lesson to attend."

Shelby glanced at her watch. She only had 25 minutes to get Mittens settled, tacked up and comfortable in the new environment. She'd better get moving!

Chapter 15

Mittens warmed up beautifully even though he was eager to look at everything in the new arena. After several laps he became comfortable in his new surroundings and was able to relax and really focus on what Shelby was asking. Allison started the group off at a posting trot, making sure everyone was keeping even spacing around the rail. She put them through the paces, asking for a sitting trot, posting trot, two-point position and finally, a halt. She told the riders to relax for a moment while she set up some ground poles.

Shelby walked Mittens to keep his muscles warm and limber. Chelsea was watching near the gate so Shelby headed over to say hello. With Arwen hurt, Chelsea and her parents had decided to go ahead and meet Socks, the Chestnut gelding. She met him for the first time last week and had really hit it off. Allison told Shelby that she wanted Chelsea to ride him one more time, but was pretty sure they had found Chelsea's new horse! Shelby was very happy for her friend.

"Shelby, he is just adorable!" Chelsea complimented Mittens. "And you do a great job riding him."

"Thanks. He's such a good pony. He makes it easy. I hear you and Socks got along famously."

Chelsea blushed, "We really did. I just really feel like we connected, you know? I'm sure it's like you and Arwen. How's she doing by the way?"

"Good! Dr. Benson is happy with how her wound is healing and said she can go out on turnout soon. Hopefully it won't be long and we will be back to jumping like we used to do!" Shelby replied.

Chelsea bit her lip, looking almost hesitant, but nodded, "Hopefully so. I really hope so."

Before Shelby could ask her what the pause meant, Allison called the lesson back to order and asked the riders to trot a small grid of ground poles with no stirrups. After everyone's legs were exhausted she gave the riders a quick walk break before putting them back on the rail to resume canter work. The riders cantered both directions of the arena, performed simple changes of lead, and worked both upward and downward transitions. The riders and horses were all practically panting when Allison finally called them into the center of the arena.

"Nice job today, everyone. I feel like we are very prepared for the show this weekend. Anyone who feels like they need one more ride before we leave for the show please find me in my office for scheduling. Nobody is allowed to ride on Thursday, okay? We will give the horses that day off before heading to the show on Friday afternoon. Got it?"

The riders all nodded and Allison continued, "Since you won't be riding on Thursday, I expect everyone will have plenty of time to make sure their equipment is clean and presentable as well as packed and ready to go. Horses are to be clipped and bathed with manes pulled. Work together, help each other, ask me any questions, and...Oh yeah, have FUN!"

Everyone laughed. A few riders asked simple questions before Allison wrapped it up.

"Be here as soon as you can after school on Friday. The horses will ship to the show Friday afternoon. We will get them settled and have a group ride after that. I expect everyone there by 6:30 on Saturday morning to get the horses ready and to support each other. Sound good? Now cool these ponies down and put them up for the night!"

Allison pulled Shelby to the side.

"Hey, Judy and I decided that it would be easiest for Mittens to stay here. He can go in Birdie's stall as she is gone for the week. We figured you'd like to ride him here another time or two and that way he can be ready to go with everyone else on Friday."

"Sweet! I'll take good care of him."

"We know you will. He looked great today."

Shelby finished walking Mittens and led him to Birdie's stall.

"You've got the prime spot," she told the pony.

Birdie, whose registered name was Badminton, was Allison's personal horse. She was a big, bay half Arabian, half Hanoverian with a huge personality. The mare was an incredible jumper and Allison was hoping she was a National contender. She was a very tough horse to ride and didn't settle easily in new places, so to practice for the upcoming competition season Allison was keeping her at a friend's barn for the week. She went and rode her every morning and it gave Birdie the experience of being ridden somewhere new. Plus it had opened up the best stall in the barn for Mittens!

Shelby found a spare blanket that would fit Mittens and tucked him in for the night. Then she and several other barn friends settled into the tack room to get a head start on cleaning tack and packing for the show.

As soon as Shelby's mom picked her up, Shelby bombarded her with the details of the day.

She told her everything she'd heard from Judy as well as how good the lesson had been.

"Well, Sage will be happy to hear that her photography skills have been so well received. Don't you dare tell her I told you this, but I think she really had fun! She went on and on about the two rescue horses that came in and how nice Judy is," Shelby's mother said.

"The secret is safe with me," Shelby giggled. "I hope I can talk her into doing it again. Even after these horses are sold and Mittens is gone, I'd still love to be involved out there."

"Well, I'm proud of you. Both of you. But there is something we need to discuss," Shelby's mothers voice took a serious tone. "I got a phone call today from Mr. Henry. He wanted to discuss your book report."

Shelby gulped. Mr. Henry was her English teacher and was known for being a tough grader. They'd recently been assigned a report, to read a book of their choice from a list of about fifty books, and do a two page typed report on how the book was relatable to their life. Shelby had chosen *Black Beauty*, by Anna Sewell for obvious reasons. It was a classic horse story. But now she wondered if her choice had been too childish and she should have chosen something else. A friend of hers had chosen *Jane Eyre*, and another, *Wuthering Heights*. Shelby thought she had written a good essay, but now she sank into her seat and prepared for a lecture on maintaining good school work.

"Shelby, Mr. Henry said he was completely surprised when he read what you had written. He said he knew you liked horses and expected as much in the essay, but everything he read left him very impressed. He said it was easily the best paper in the whole class! I'm so proud of you, honey!"

Shelby breathed a sigh of relief. She'd been so worried that she had failed the report. And to hear that Mr. Henry had loved it, what a shock! She wasn't about to admit to her mother that the main reason she'd chosen Black Beauty, aside from it being a horse book, was because Shelby knew she would be able to write that essay quickly and be done with the assignment. Now, to hear that it had been so well received was astounding, but she'd take it!

"I called your father to share the good news. He's very proud of you, too. He's picking up Chinese food, your favorite, for dinner so we can celebrate. Great job!"

"Thanks, Mom!" Shelby grinned, vowing that she would start to really put in more of an effort into her English class. Think of how well she could do if she was really trying!

Later that night, after feasting with her family on sesame chicken and eggrolls, Shelby was in her room going over her science notes when there was a knock at the door. Her mother entered holding a small gift bag.

"I'd already picked this out for you because I've just been so proud of you lately. You've handled the situation with Arwen so gracefully. And now you are volunteering at the rescue and doing so many great things over there. The phone call from your teacher was just the icing on the cake. I know you are excited about this weekend. I thought this might make you stand out a bit."

She handed Shelby the package and Shelby carefully removed its contents. Inside was a beautiful pale blue checkered riding shirt with a monogrammed collar. It would match her hunt coat perfectly and would be a beautiful color on both Arwen and Mittens. She'd always just shown in a plain white shirt that had been passed down from an older rider at the barn. The new shirt was very sharp.

"Thanks, Mom!" she said as she hugged her mother. "It's perfect!"

"Well, you needed a new one, something a little fancier. I thought the blue was pretty. Dad and I are looking forward to watching you show this weekend. We know you'll do great!"

Shelby's mom stepped out of the room and closed the door to let Shelby finish studying. Shelby hung her new shirt on a hanger next to her hunt coat and tried to focus on science.

Chapter 16

Shelby arrived at the rescue Thursday afternoon eager to play with Gatsby. She'd worked hard the last few days preparing Mittens for the show. He was clipped and his mane was pulled. All that was left to do was to give him a quick bath this afternoon and pack the saddle in the trailer. Everything else was packed and ready.

Shelby was excited to see Allison's truck at the rescue when she arrived. Allison had told her that she would take a look at Gatsby's papers and try to track down any information she could find on him.

Allison was in the barn showing Capone to a friend of hers who did three day eventing.

"He's fantastic," her friend, Meg, was saying. "Hey, Shelby! Thanks for finally making Allison share this horse with the rest of us!"

"Ha, ha!" Allison replied. "He wasn't ready to go yet, but he is now. So, what do you think?"

"I think he'll be perfect! He's bold and almost a little ornery. I like that," Meg grinned. "Plus he's got good confirmation and big, sturdy bones. I think he'll make a nice event prospect. I'd love to take him, unless of course, you want him for yourself?"

"Oh, no! I've got enough on my plate. Come on, we'll go work out all the details with Judy. But first, Shelby, let me fill you in on what I found out about Gatsby. His name is SGF Great Gatsby. The SGF stands for his breeder, Stone Gate Farm. He's very well bred. He's ten years old and actually has a show record. It looks like he was started in hunter pleasure and then also did some jumping. It shows he was jumping two feet at the shows, but that was four years ago. I'm trying to track down his old trainer from somewhere in Kansas or Missouri. He's traveled a good distance! As I put more together I will let you know, but knew you'd like to know this. It looks like he did okay when he was showing. He didn't win a bunch, but he earned some ribbons and it's nice to know he has some experience."

Shelby thanked Allison then headed to greet her buddy. A registered purebred Arabian! And with a show record in jumping! Shelby knew that with that kind of information and as well connected as Allison was with the Arabian horse people, they should eventually be able to find a great home for the horse. But Shelby hoped it wouldn't be any time too soon.

She slipped the halter over his head and snapped on a lead rope. Grooming him was much easier than the first time, but Shelby still did an extra thorough job. She could tell he was already much shinier than when he'd first arrived. His feet looked much better after a visit from the farrier, too. When he was all groomed, Shelby found a lunge line and a whip in the tack room. Lunging was a ground exercise where the person stood in the middle of the circle. The horse, attached to the lunge line, performed his gaits on the outside of the circle. It was a tool used for both training and exercise. The lunge whip was not used as punishment, but more of a guide to encourage and direct the horse where to go.

She led Gatsby out to the arena to begin their work. She figured that since he had pretty extensive prior training he would at least know how to lunge. As she hooked up the lunge line and clucked to him, she was happy to see that her hunch was correct. Gatsby calmly walked in a circle around her. She gave him plenty of time to walk and get comfortable both directions before clucking to him and asking him to trot.

Gatsby reached forward into a smooth, floating trot. He had a big ground covering stride and a swinging step. He stretched his body gracefully as a trotted around the circle.

All of a sudden, he exploded. He leapt forward on the lunge line at a full gallop, bucking and snorting. Shelby froze, terrified that he was going to pull away from her. She was glad that she'd been smart enough to put the chain around his nose as a precaution. It could be used to help slow him down. Shelby quickly snapped back into gear and began telling the horse to "Woah" in a calm voice. She tugged gently on the rope. As quickly as it had happened, Gatsby stopped his shenanigans and continued trotting in the circle like it had never happened. Shelby realized that he'd never even really tried to pull away from her. It was just as though he had a lot of pent up energy that he needed to get out.

She worked him at a trot several minutes before reversing direction and trotting him again. She made sure to give him plenty of breaks to walk. She knew that a horse as out of shape as he was would tire quickly. Gatsby never took another wrong step. He acted like a perfect gentleman.

As a treat to Gatsby at the end of their session, Shelby decided to take him for a little walk. She walked him in between the lanes of the paddocks and up and down the driveway, letting him pause to nibble bits of grass and sniff the leaves. Gatsby was thrilled with the green grass and enjoyed meeting some of his new equine buddies over the fence.

After returning Gatsby to his stall and giving him a quick brushing, Shelby decided to share some of her love with Roman and got the old horse out and allowed him to graze in the stable yard. She brushed his coat and untangled his mane. She wasn't sure but it looked as though Roman had already gained a little weight in the week he'd been at the rescue. His attitude had certainly improved! He nuzzled at Shelby and tugged at the lead rope to get at the most tender pieces of clover that were just out of his reach. Finally, after he'd had his fill of grass, the old horse just stood in the sun, closing his eyes and enjoying being lavished with attention.

Chapter 17

The day before the show arrived, it was warm and sunny and Shelby and Taylor waited impatiently for school to let out for the weekend. Finally they arrived at the farm and gathered with other riding students to finish all of the last minute show preparations to head to the horse show.

Allison had already taken the first load of horses to the show grounds and was returning with the trailer to get the final four.

Mittens, Mercury, Avenue and Top Hat were groomed to perfection and ready to go. As Taylor double checked to make sure enough feed had been packed, Shelby and another riding student, Hailey, did a final sweep through the tack room to make sure nothing had been forgotten.

"What about these earplugs?" Hailey asked referring to little pompom like plugs that could be put in the ears of a very nervous horse to help block out some of the noise.

Shelby shrugged, "We probably don't need them since Bridie's not going to this show, but I guess it can't hurt to bring them along just in case."

When it came to horse shows, Shelby tended to be of the mindset of over-packing instead of getting to a show and wishing you had packed something.

Shelby picked up a standing martingale. "I decided I better bring this, too. I haven't been using it on Mittens, but I'd like to have one just in case he gets a little too excited in a show atmosphere."

A martingale was a piece of tack worn by a horse or pony to prevent him from being able to reach his head excessively high and thus avoiding direction from a rider. Shelby hoped Mittens wouldn't need it, but she wanted to have one if she needed it so she put it in the tack box.

"Cute little Mittens!" Hailey said. "Is he really for sale?"

"He is. Are you looking?" Shelby asked, surprised. Hailey was super nice, but she'd only just been riding about as long as Taylor. She was showing in the crossrail division too. Shelby wasn't quite sure she was ready for a horse of her own.

"For me? Oh no, of course not. My cousin might be though. You remember Savannah, right? She got me started in horses."

Shelby did remember Savannah. She'd come out several times to watch lessons and hang out with Hailey. She lived about an hour away from the High Lane Farm, so she rode at a stable in her town. But Shelby remembered that the ten year old was incredibly talented on a horse. And she seemed very passionate about it. Shelby had liked her instantly.

"Savannah's getting a horse? That's cool." Shelby replied.

"Well, they're looking. She finally talked her dad into it," Hailey laughed. "I told her about Mittens, I hope that's okay. He fits a lot of the criteria they are looking for."

"No, that's great. I think it would be a good match," Shelby said honestly.

"Their barn is going to be at the show so Savannah will be there tomorrow. She's not showing, but she's coming to cheer for her friends and maybe see Mittens."

"Yeah, definitely bring her over to meet him! Hey, I think I hear the trailer. Let's go load the last of this stuff so we can get to the show."

After all of the horses had been settled with fresh shavings, full water buckets and a flake of hay in their stalls, the group quickly unpacked the trailer and set up an extra stall as a makeshift tack room. All of the tack was sorted and hung on hooks to make it easily accessible the next day. Horse shows always tended to include moments of panic where someone couldn't find their helmet or needed a crop, so the High Lane group made sure to stay as organized as possible.

Allison then went over the schedule. Some of the lesson horses would have two riders so she asked the more experienced riders to be sure to help the others. Then she instructed everyone to tack up for a quick ride to acclimate the horses to the new arena.

Mittens came out of his stall much more excited than Shelby had ever seen him. His ears swiveled frantically and his eyes were wide as he took in his new surroundings.

"There now. Easy boy," Shelby cooed to him as she and the other riders led their horses to the arena. "It's just show jitters."

Mittens danced and wouldn't be still at the mounting block, so finally Allison had to hold him for Shelby to climb on.

"You sure you can handle him?" Allison asked concerned.

Shelby nodded but she wasn't sure. She hoped he didn't get any more excited.

The pony pranced around the arena, shying at jumps and barely paying attention to Shelby. After one lap, Allison stopped them.

"Go ahead and hop down. I sent Hailey back to the tack stall to get a lunge line and a martingale. She said you packed an extra? Smart thinking. Lunge him for a bit and we'll try again. Remember, we don't know what his past show experience was."

When Hailey got back with the lunge line, Shelby led Mittens to the designated lunging area and adjusted his tack so it was safer for lunging. The pony raced around on the lunge line, putting on quite a show. When he finally started to slow down on his own, Shelby halted him and hand walked him for a while. He was dripping with sweat but at least his eyes weren't quite so wide anymore.

Allison walked over to help her adjust the martingale and hold him for Shelby to mount.

"He seems a little better now, huh?" Allison mused. "Don't worry. Take your time tonight. Just walk him around the arena, let him see everything. Everyone else is done so I'm going to send them back to the barn to untack and do chores."

Allison hurried away and Shelby began allowing Mittens to walk cautiously around the arena. She decided to let him walk by the jumps to see them. As she turned to walk to the first jump, she looked up and wanted to crawl in a hole. There, standing at the red oxer jump, was Mrs. Marsh, Corinna, and their spectacular new horse. The two were talking while the chestnut stood on a loose rein looking like the packer that he was.

Shelby thought about changing direction right as Mrs. Marsh look up.

"Shelby!" she declared. "Hello! That's quite an exciting ride you've got there."

Apparently, they'd witnessed the whole thing. Shelby tried to keep an even tone, but having the Marshes watch her struggle just added to the humiliation.

"Yeah, he got a little over excited, but I think he's better now," she said.

"So is he a new lesson pony for Allison? He seems awfully hot to be a lesson pony!" Mrs. Marsh asserted.

"No, he's not for lessons. I'm riding him for Judy at Hoofed Hearts Equine Rescue. He's for sale."

"A rescue? Oh that's sweet. I'm sure he'll make a nice little pleasure pony for someone."

Shelby held back her infuriation. This "little pleasure pony" had been a show champion in his past. But there was no use in wasting her energy trying to explain that to Mrs. Marsh. Besides, she'd already started prattling on again.

"Well, Galileo here was quite a good boy, so we need to be getting him untacked and taken care of. Hopefully, your little pony will settle down a little. See you tomorrow, dear."

Then she and Corinna led the horse towards the out gate and back to the stalls. Shelby tried to think positive thoughts, like beating Corinna and Galileo, as she continued to work Mittens. He'd calmed down considerably, but still wasn't quite as in tune with his rider as he was at home. Allison arrived and gave her some pointers and exercises and finally they reached a point where both trainer and rider thought it was time to call it a night. Mittens had taken several good laps around the arena, had jumped all the fences and had taken several very good lines. It was best to put him up before he got grouchy.

After Mittens was cool, Shelby dismounted to walk back to the stable with Allison.

"I saw you talking to Mrs. Marsh. I know she gets to you, but don't worry about anything she says. She just loves to see Corinna win no matter who she has to put down to get there."

"Corinna doesn't even seem to care about horses!" Shelby cried.

Allison shrugged. "Maybe, who knows? All that really matters is you and Mittens. He calmed down there at the end. I think you'll be fine. Tomorrow he'll be back to his old self, you'll see."

Shelby got a mischievous look in her eye and said, "Good, then we can set about beating Corinna and the wonder horse."

Chapter 18

It was still dark when Taylor's mom dropped the girls at the show grounds the next morning. Taylor and Shelby made their way to the stalls and began to help feed. Each rider was responsible for taking care of their own horse or pony at the show, including feeding and cleaning stalls. But usually the High Lane Farm riders pitched in and worked together to get the job done.

When the work was done, everyone gathered in the small tack stall for a pep talk.

"Score!" Shelby said taking a donut from the box of warm, fresh donuts that one of the adult riders had brought along to share. "Thanks, Susan!"

"No problem!" Susan grinned. "We need some sugar to get us going this early in the morning."

"Alright, alright. Let's get this show on the road," Allison joked. Everyone groaned as she continued, "What? Too early for bad jokes? Tough crowd this morning! Have the horses all been fed, watered and have clean stalls?"

Everyone nodded.

"Great, let's get Top Hat, Mercury and Kineer out for quick hand walk. It doesn't need to be long but the older guys need to stretch. Susan and I are going to finish braiding the last two. Shelby, I think you should take Mittens down to the arena to lunge. Try to keep him at a trot so he doesn't get to tired and sweaty, but use your best judgment. If he's a bundle of energy, let him get it out, okay? Everyone else can tidy up and make sure everything is ready to go."

Everyone started going in the direction they'd been told. Shelby grabbed a lunge line and lunge whip and headed towards Mitten's stall. She was a little apprehensive to get him out and see how hyped up he was, but it had to be done.

Luckily, Mittens walked out of his stall acting like his old self. He was calm and even yawned lazily in the aisle as Shelby ran a brush over him and wrapped his legs. Of course, Shelby knew the true test would come when they got closer to the show ring, especially now that other riders and horses were starting to warm up. But Mittens walked like a gentleman to the arena and seemed totally unfazed by everything going on around him. Shelby lunged him at a trot until she was sure the pony had had plenty of time to get out any silliness. Then she walked him back to the stalls to get him ready for the show ring.

The stabling area was bustling when Shelby returned. All around, horses were being braided, hooves were being oiled and tack was being polished. Shelby put Mittens in his stall and searched for Allison to see what she could do to be helpful. The beginner classes would start first, with the jumping classes later in the morning and in the afternoon. Shelby's parents would show up around lunchtime, after Tucker's karate class. Shelby knew they were bringing sandwiches, fruit salad, pasta salad and her dad's famous brownies!

"Shelby!" Allison panted, "Find Taylor and Hailey and start tacking up the beginner horses please. The starting time is sneaking up on us! How was Mittens?"

"He was good and much calmer than yesterday."

"See, I told you. We'll be sure to give you plenty of warm up before your class. I'm heading to the show office but I'll be back in a minute."

Shelby found Taylor and Hailey putting some tack away and told them their assignment. At home, riders were responsible for tacking up their own horses, but at shows everyone pitched in to help each other. That way, the rider showing could focus on getting dressed in their show clothes without getting covered in horse hair and slobber!

The girls worked together tacking up each horse and putting on the finishing touches. They brushed out tails, used baby wipes to clean their eyes and noses, and brushed finishing spray on their coats to make them shine. Clean white saddle pads and well-oiled saddles were placed on their backs. Then the horses were tied in the stalls to wait for their riders.

One by one the riders came out of the tack stall dressed and ready to go. A few of the riders looked excited but most of them looked a little nervous. The older girls tried to calm their show fears by sharing their first horse show experience. They let on that they still got nervous too, especially Taylor and Hailey who were still very new to this as well.

Allison helped bridle the three horses, and the riders and horses headed to the arena for the beginner walk trot classes. The classes were divided by age group and were kept small to give the riders confidence and keep everyone safe.

"Can you guys tack up your crossrail horses and get dressed? Chelsea and Susan are at the arena to help me, but I can send one of them up if you think you'll need help." Allison asked the girls.

"Oh, no. We'll be fine. I can get the horses ready while Taylor and Hailey get dressed." Shelby replied.

Allison nodded and left to meet her riders at the arena. Taylor and Hailey thanked Shelby and headed behind the curtained tack stall to get changed into show clothes.

Shelby got Avenue ready first. The big chestnut gelding was a retired saddle seat horse who had found a new career as a low level jumper. He was half Arab, half Saddlebred and had big long legs to get over the jumps but he was very careful and took good care of his riders.

Next she got Midas cleaned up. Grey horses were hard to keep clean, but Shelby had seen Hailey brushing him earlier in the morning so he wasn't that hard to get ready. She was just about to saddle, when a familiar face appeared outside the stall door.

"Judy! I'm glad you came!" Shelby exclaimed.

"Well, I couldn't miss your debut with Mittens, could I?" she teased.

Judy helped saddle Midas while filling Shelby in on everything that had been going on at the rescue.

"Allison's friend, Meg, just loves Capone and she is going to pick him up tomorrow. I really like her, so I'm excited to see what they will accomplish together. And the family I told you about, with the little boy? They came to see Mischief last night and he and the boy just hit it off. So they are buying him."

She went on to say that a lady had come out to ride Sally and really liked her. She was an older lady, whose last horse had died at age 27. She loved having a horse around and would trail ride with friends about once a week. It sounded like the ideal situation for Sally. The lady wanted to come ride her one more time and bring a friend to see her but the situation was promising.

"So in a week, we've got three new owners or potential owners! I'm so grateful. Now the rescue can continue to help other horses in need," Judy thanked Shelby.

Hailey and Taylor showed up dressed and ready to go. Shelby gave them a quick once over, adjusting hair and wiping boots, then they grabbed the horses and all headed to the ring together. It was show time!

Chapter 19

Taylor was trotting around the ring looking confident until the judge called a sitting trot. Shelby knew that Avenue had a very bouncy trot that was hard to sit.

"You look fine! Smile!" she told her friend as she passed.

"And back to the posting trot," the announcer said. This was the flat class before the crossrails classes. There were eight riders in the class performing at a walk, trot and canter on the rail.

"Pick up the canter, please. Canter!" the microphone boomed.

Shelby saw Hailey cue Midas to canter but unfortunately she wasn't very definite when she asked and he picked up the wrong lead. She saw Allison grimace from across the arena. Shelby was closest to Hailey so as she got close, Shelby whispered loudly "Switch your lead!"

Hailey glanced down and realized she was wrong. She slowed Midas and asked for the canter again and this time he picked it up correctly.

The rest of the class went well for both riders.

The announcer called them to line up in the center of the ring and they all trotted in.

"First place goes to Charlotte Watson, riding Mystery."

Shelby clapped politely as a rider from another farm accepted the blue ribbon.

"Second place is Taylor Snyder, riding Park Avenue."

"Woohoo!" Shelby cheered as Taylor's mother clapped loudly beside her.

Taylor came out of the arena grinning from ear to ear and petting Avenue.

"Great job, buddy!" she told him. "That was so fun!"

Hailey ended up fourth, probably because of the lead. But she seemed content and ready to focus on the next phase of showing... the crossrails!

Shelby's parents arrived just in time to see Taylor's last class. Altogether in the crossrails division, Taylor received a first, a third, and a fourth. She was over the moon with excitement. Mrs. Snyder took about a thousand pictures with her ribbons before Taylor took the big gelding back to the barn to be put away.

Shelby was starting to get a little nervous. She hoped Mittens would listen to her so they would put in a good showing. She really wanted to do well so he could find a great home. And Judy and Allison had been so nice. She just wanted to make them proud.

"Shelby, you need to eat something!" her dad said. "Come get a sandwich. I've got it all set up."

Her parents had set up a folding table back at the stalls with all sorts of food on it. Shelby fixed a small plate, knowing that she wouldn't be able to eat much. She sat in a chair outside Mittens stall and went over the jump course in her head. There were a few tricky spots and one jump that Mittens had been very weary of yesterday. Shelby knew that the more she rode it in her head, the more confident she would be in the saddle.

After the lunch break, Allison was back at the arena with two of the riders doing the two foot hunter division. Shelby went to get dressed while Taylor and Chelsea tacked up Mittens. Her new show shirt made her look very polished and Shelby was glad she'd stayed up late last night shining her boots. She looked like she was ready to win!

When they got down to the arena, Mittens appeared to be calm and focused. Shelby waved to her parents who were sitting with Judy by the arena watching classes, then she got to work. Chelsea held Mittens while Shelby pulled down her stirrups and mounted. Taylor gave her boots a wipe down with a towel. Shelby walked Mittens all over, letting him stretch and see everything. Then she put him to work asking him to trot and canter around the practice ring. She was happy to find that Mittens appeared to be cool and collected. They were ready to show!

The first class was an equitation class on the flat. Equitation judges riders on their posture and ability to ride. Of course, Shelby knew that the horse still played a large role in the placing of an equitation class. A horse that was running around being naughty certainly didn't help the rider look very good!

The class was going great until they reversed direction. Mittens was trotting when all of a sudden he shied violently at something outside the arena. Shelby stayed on and managed to get him back under control, but she knew the judge had seen it and it would count against them. Still, she reminded herself that this class was just a warmup for her other classes. And she was happy when she got fourth place out of nine riders. It showed that the judge still thought she had done a good job in spite of the spook. Corinna won the class and Shelby could see why. Her new horse never seemed to put a hoof wrong. He was like a horse show machine.

The next class was the first section of hunter over fences at 2'6". Shelby entered at a walk and picked up a smooth canter for her courtesy circle. She made sure to apply plenty of inside leg and hold her outside rein when they passed the spot he'd shied at earlier. Allison had told her to be prepared and to respond that way. Luckily, Mittens cantered on, as if he knew they were ready to jump. He soared over the fences, even the one he had been scared of yesterday. He did seem to jump that one just a bit higher than the rest, though. He performed perfect flying lead changes when asked and hit all the correct strides. Shelby was thrilled. She flung her arms around his neck as soon as they'd exited the arena.

"Good boy! You were such a good boy!" she smooched in his ear. "I'm so proud of you!"

"Way to go Shelby!" Allison said rushing over and patting the pony. "I don't care how you place! That round was amazing!"

Shelby beamed but gave credit to her pony. "Oh, he's the amazing one. He just went out there and did his job."

"Look, you've got some fans," Allison said, pointing to where her parents were sitting and saw that Hailey was sitting there with her cousin, Savannah. Savannah grinned and waved and gave her a thumb- up. Shelby knew she had to be impressed with the pony after a ride like that.

Shelby heard Corinna's name being called and turned to watch her enter the arena on the chestnut horse. The round started well, but it went downhill from there. Her new horse was a good jumper, but he appeared to be very strong. After the third fence, Corinna tried to do a change of lead, but he was going too fast and strong to listen to her. She finally got it changed but his stride was off and he had to leap over the fourth fence. After that, the ride went better although it never really seemed like Corinna was in control.

"What was that?" Mrs. Marsh demanded as Corinna came out of the ring. "He was all over the place. Why didn't you slow him down?"

"I tried, mother. He's too strong. Put a different bit in his mouth," Corinna said, dismounting and flinging the reins at her mother.

"Yikes!" Taylor whispered. "I wouldn't want to ride in that car on the way home."

"No kidding. That's a nice horse, but they need a lot of work," Shelby replied.

"Guess that means there's a better chance at you winning," Taylor said slyly.

"Hopefully so!" Shelby grinned.

The rest of Shelby's hunter rounds went just as well as the first and she ended up winning three blue ribbons for her over fences classes and a second place in her hunter pleasure class. Word had gotten around about Mitten's past as a rescue pony and everywhere Shelby went she was met with congratulations. Judy was so proud and wouldn't stop grinning.

"This seems like one special pony!" Savannah said, finally getting a chance to talk to Shelby as she cooled down Mittens.

"He absolutely is! Are you going to come try him?" Shelby asked.

"I am!" Savannah responded excitedly, "My parents talked to Judy and we are going to come ride him this week. We were all impressed with what we saw today. You've done a great job with him."

"Thanks. He's been really fun. Do you want to walk him and get to know him a little?" Shelby asked, glancing at Savannah.

"Yes! Come here boy," Savannah whispered to the pony, " I just know we're going to be great friends."

As she left Mittens with Savannah to go find something to drink, Shelby passed Mrs. Marsh who was cooling down Corinna's horse. She smiled, tight lipped at Shelby, but continued walking. Corinna's rounds had gotten better after they had put a stronger bit in the horse's mouth, but they were far from perfect. Shelby figured Mrs. Marsh was questioning whether they'd bought the right horse for Corinna.

Shelby grabbed a bottle of water and downed about half of it. The jump crew was in the arena raising the fences for the higher jump classes. Shelby wanted to get Mittens and get him all taken care of so she could come back and watch some more classes. The more advanced classes were so exciting!

Suddenly the announcer came over the loudspeaker, "We have the division champions for the 2'6" hunter division. Reserve Champion goes to Mackenzie Walsh, riding Hello Kitty. And your Champion is Shelby Davies, riding Snow Mittens. Congratulations!"

In a blur, Shelby was surrounded by her friends and family. Everyone congratulated and hugged her. Savannah brought Mittens over and handed him to Shelby as someone fastened a big Champion ribbon to his bridle. Taylor's mom was taking pictures so the whole High Lane Farm group got together for a big group photo. Shelby hugged Mitten's neck and kissed him on the nose. This was the best day ever!

Chapter 20

Shelby ran to the barn after getting off the bus on Tuesday afternoon. She was still floating on air after the horse show and she couldn't wait to get to the barn. Allison had called her yesterday to say that Savannah, her parents and her trainer were coming to ride Mittens this afternoon. If they liked him they would be taking him on trial for a few weeks to make sure they got along.

Shelby was really going to miss the pony, but she knew he'd be going to an excellent home. She really couldn't ask for more. Besides, she'd known that riding him was only temporary until he was sold or Arwen got better.

Shelby saw that a trailer she didn't recognize was parked by the barn and figured it belonged to Savannah's trainer. Sure enough, she caught a glimpse of the little gray pony soaring over some jumps in the arena. She hurried to go watch.

Mittens and Savannah seemed to be getting along famously. Shelby knew that a talented rider like Savannah would appreciate this pony and his sense of humor. Mittens pranced as Savannah tried to slow him to a walk and tossed his head in protest. Clearly he wanted to jump more fences, but Savannah just laughed and patted him on the neck.

"Silly pony! Hey Shelby," she called cheerfully. "This pony is a dream. And such a clown, too."

She rode the pony over next to Shelby and halted.

"So, do you like him?" Shelby asked.

"I do! I love him. And if I have anything to say about it he'll be getting on the trailer to go home with me," Savannah said, then she got quiet. "Are you sure about this? Won't you miss him?"

"Well, sure I'll miss him, but my job was always just to find him a good home. And I couldn't think of a better one than you. Besides,

Arwen will be better soon and I'll get to go back to jumping her."

Relief washed over Savannah's face. "Phew! Okay. I felt so guilty, like I was taking your horse away. Well, then yes, if you are sure then I definitely want this pony and promise to give him the best home ever!"

Savannah flung her arms around Mittens. Her dad walked over and laughed. "I take it you might like him?" he teased. "I guess that means he's coming home with us?"

Savannah squeaked and Shelby grinned. She knew Mitten's life as a downtrodden rescue pony was over forever and he'd be loved for the rest of his life.

Shelby and Savannah took care of Mittens while the adults worked out all of the details in Allison's office. Judy had approved a two week trial, just in case but Shelby knew that Mitten's had found his forever home. She and Savannah gathered up some feed for him, prepared a hay bag for the ride to the new stable and carefully wrapped his legs.

Finally, it was time to say goodbye. Savannah gave Shelby a few minutes alone with Mittens in his stall.

"Thanks for keeping my spirits up while Arwen was hurt. We had a great time, didn't we buddy? I'll always remember riding you to my very first championship ribbon," she murmured while stroking the pony's forelock. He butted against her begging for treats. She hugged him one last time then left the stall allowing Judy a chance to say her final goodbyes.

Judy came out of the stall misty eyed but she smiled happily at Savannah as she handed her the lead rope.

"This is why I do what I do," she explained. "It's hard work and very sad sometimes but in the end, if I can help make happy moments like these, then it's all worth it. Now go load your new pony!"

Goodbyes were exchanged and Mittens loaded on the trailer like a pro. As the truck and trailer pulled away, Judy put her arms around

Allison and Shelby and said, "We make a pretty good team, you know?"

Shelby and Judy stood outside and made arrangements for Shelby to come work Gatsby later in the week. Then Judy left, so Shelby wandered back into the barn planning to visit with Arwen and clean her tack left from the horse show. Allison stopped her in the aisle.

"Can we talk?" she said quietly.

"Sure. What's up?" Shelby immediately sensed that something was wrong, but she couldn't think of what it would be.

Allison closed the office door behind her and sat down. Shelby sank into the couch.

"I don't know how to tell you this," Allison started, "Especially after the incredible weekend you had. I don't want to ruin that, but..."

"What? Spit it out," Shelby demanded.

"Dr. Benson came and evaluated Arwen again this morning. There have been some concerns we've both been having. Now that the wounds are getting better and the swelling is down he could really do a better evaluation. Shelby, Arwen is lame. She's never going to get better. She has a small bone chip and the wound caused so much damage to her leg that she's going to have arthritis. I'm so sorry."

Shelby sat there, stunned. In the beginning she'd thought that Arwen not getting better was a possibility, but the past few weeks had been so positive that Shelby just assumed everything was fine.

"What are you saying?" Shelby asked, bewildered.

"Shelby, we can't ride Arwen anymore. We can't jump her. She can't do anything strenuous," Allison explained.

"So... what? What are you going to do with her?" Shelby cried hysterically.

"What do you mean?" Allison looked puzzled, then it clicked. "Oh, no! You thought we were going to put her down. No! No, of course not. She can live here, hang out, we just won't be able to ride her."

Shelby took a deep breath. She was relieved, but very sad at the same time. "So, I can't ride her, like, ever again?"

Allison shook her head sadly. "No, I'm afraid not. She's not going to be in pain and she'll be able to happily run around the pastures, but riding would just be too much added weight and stress."

"So what will she do?" Shelby asked incredulously.

"I've thought about breeding her. A little Arwen baby might be fun. I don't really know yet."

"Oh, okay." Shelby paused for a long time.

"I'm going to go check on her," she said finally as she quickly headed out the door. She fled to Arwen's stall, ignoring Allison's concerned calls.

Arwen was in her stall so Shelby sank into her favorite spot under the feeder and cried. The mare snuffled at her curiously.

Shelby had been so happy for Savannah and Mittens just minutes earlier, but now she realized what it meant for her situation. She had just lost both of her riding horses in the same day. First, Mittens being sold and now the realization that Arwen would never go back to work. Shelby had no horse to ride.

Sure, there were plenty of nice school horses at High Lane Farm. They were all pretty, suitable for different levels of riders and were talented and capable horses. But they were all school horses. They were ridden and loved by many riders a week. What Shelby had found so great about Arwen was that she was able to develop such a bond with the mare. She was practically the only one to ride her, so they knew and understood each other. That's what riding had meant to Shelby lately. She loved having a relationship with one special horse. And now that was gone.

"At least I can still brush you and love you," she sniffled to Arwen. "And I'll come and feed you treats."

She knew the mare would be fine. And she would always love Arwen and have a special place in her heart for the horse. But with Arwen lame, who would Shelby ride? Who would she focus all of her riding energy into?

"At least there's Gatsby," she thought, but then she remembered that he, too, would be sold. She wondered if she should even get attached.

Shelby sat pondering her situation until it was time for her to go and she ran out into the parking lot to meet her mother.

Chapter 21

Shelby ended up going to the rescue almost every day after school that week. Allison called her, concerned that she hadn't been out to High Lane Farm all week, but Shelby just told her that she was busy with Gatsby. It was the truth but she also needed some time to process her thoughts.

Spending time at the rescue just confirmed what Shelby already knew. She loved horses. She was totally horse crazy and just because she'd had some bad luck lately didn't mean she would give up on riding. She'd had some great luck, too, like meeting Judy and Mittens and winning her first championship. She was coming to realize that life with horses was full of ups and downs. But if you really, truly loved it you stuck with it and pressed forward.

Gatsby was amazing and as much as Shelby tried not to, she had grown very attached to the dark bay gelding. He was really something special. He was starting to blossom under Shelby's love and attention. With all of the good grooming, exercise, and proper nutrition he was beginning to look like the beautiful horse that he was.

Shelby went out to the rescue Saturday morning. She had decided that today would be the day that she put a saddle on Gatsby. Even though Gatsby had been ridden in the past, no one knew quite how he would handle being saddled and ridden so it was best to take it one step at a time. If the lunging with a saddle proved to be no big deal, then Shelby would continue with the training process and maybe start riding him soon!

She got Gatsby out of his stall and groomed him in the crossties, chatting with him the whole time. The horse listened attentively with his ears perked, nodding every now and then as if to agree. Shelby carefully wrapped his legs with polo wraps and gathered all the tack she needed and put it in the arena. She decided to put the saddle on in the arena in case he got nervous. She had seen Allison start many horses this way. If they got nervous, it was much safer to have them run around on a lunge line than to be stuck in a stall with them.

Judy came out to help as promised. She would hold Gatsby while Shelby placed the saddle on his back. They let Gatsby inspect the tack that was sitting on the fence waiting for him, then Shelby lunged him for a few minutes. She used the same routine she always did so everything would be calm and familiar for him.

Finally they felt like it was time. Judy held the lunge rope while Shelby patted and praised the horse and slowly lifted a saddle pad to his back. Gatsby didn't even flinch. Shelby reached for the saddle and allowed Gatsby to sniff it before placing it on top of the pad. She carefully did the girth and then took the lunge rope from Judy. They both stood back, waiting to see what was next. Gatsby didn't even seem to notice that he had been saddled. Shelby took him to the center of the arena and asked him to trot. He trotted and even cantered just as calm and cool as ever.

Judy finally said, "Well, he certainly doesn't seem to mind this, does he?"

Shelby shook her head. She halted Gatsby and led him over to Judy. "Will you hold him so I can put weight in the stirrups? I just want to see if he reacts."

Judy eyed her suspiciously, but she took the lunge line. "You be careful," she warned.

Shelby grabbed her helmet and the mounting block and carried it over to Gatsby. She put a little weight in the stirrup and leaned over the saddle. She had seen Allison do this before. Gatsby glanced at her and gave a bored sigh.

"Can I get on?" she asked Judy.

Judy pointed her finger at her. "Just so you know, I think this is a bad idea!" she teased.

Shelby grinned, "But you're going to let me do it anyways, aren't you?"

"Yes, go for it. He seems fine. Be slow and cautious."

Shelby bounced on the mounting block for a few seconds before springing lightly onto Gatsby's back and settling in the saddle.

Gatsby took a tentative step forward to adjust to the additional weight. He was clearly unimpressed with the whole exercise and didn't seem to understand why his people were making such a fuss over something he clearly already knew.

Judy led him forward at the walk and decided to lunge Gatsby with Shelby riding him. This way Shelby could practice steering and halting and get a feel for the horse while giving him a refresher as well.

After a while Shelby asked, "Do you think I could trot him?"

Judy contemplated, "I guess so. Just be cautious."

Shelby didn't wait for her to change her mind. She took a firm grip on the reins and cued Gatsby lightly to trot. He sprang forward in a bold, ground covering trot. Shelby felt like she was floating. She half halted lightly, asking the horse to collect up underneath her, unsure of how he would respond. He lifted his back and arched his neck into a beautiful collected gait. He had a great rhythm to his posting trot. He marched forward with his ears perked, clearly enjoying being back to work.

"Wow! That's beautiful!" Judy called out.

"It feels magnificent!" Shelby exclaimed. She stroked Gatsby's neck.

After two more laps, Shelby sank into her heels and sat deep in the saddle. Gatsby responded by slowing to a walk and finally a halt. He'd had a big day and Shelby didn't want to overwhelm him and tire him out. Judy held his bridle while Shelby quietly dismounted then she threw her arms around the horse, praising him.

"I didn't know what to expect from today, but I certainly didn't expect that," Judy admitted.

Shelby was shocked, too. She hadn't expected the horse to be so well trained, have such a lovely trot and be so light in the bridle. Her feelings for him had tripled. The horse was overwhelmingly nice. Shelby figured he may still have some rough spots, but so far he was a really good boy.

"I think we'll call it a day," she told Gatsby.

He had worked up a little bit of a sweat so Shelby took some time to make sure he was cooled down. She brushed him and turned him out in a big grass paddock, watching him roll as soon as she closed the gate. Then she hurried to say goodbye to Judy. Her mom was picking her up to go trail riding with Taylor and she didn't want to be late.

Chapter 22

The following Saturday, Shelby got ready to go to the barn. Her parents said that they would drop her off on their way to the store.

At the barn Shelby hopped out of the car and saw her parents getting out, too.

"You don't have to stay. I'm fine," she told them.

"Oh, we want to come in and say hi to Allison. We haven't seen her since the show," her mother said.

They all walked into the barn together. Allison, Judy and Taylor were gathered in front of one of the stalls.

"Hi guys! What's going on?" Shelby asked.

Everyone, including her parents started glancing at each other.

Finally, her mother spoke, "Shelby, we know how much riding means to you, and how devastated you were after going through everything with Arwen. And we understand now how dedicated you are to all of this, and how talented you are, too. So when Judy and Allison brought this up, we took some time to think about it. It's going to require you to work really hard. And you have to keep your grades up, but we know you can do it."

Shelby looked at her bewildered, "What are you saying?"

Her dad continued, "What your mother is trying to say is that Gatsby is yours now. He's your horse!"

Just then Gatsby threw his elegant head over the stall door and whinnied loudly.

"What? Really?" Shelby cried going over to the horse and grabbing his head in her hands. "He's mine? Mine?"

Her father laughed and her mother wiped tears away. "Yes, all yours. It's a lot of responsibility but we know you are capable of it."

"Thank you! Thank you!" Shelby sobbed hugging her parents.

"Don't thank us. Allison and Judy were the real miracle workers here."

Judy spoke up, "There is no one I would rather give this horse to than you. Besides, you've already worked so hard for me to get those horses sold, I owe you this. But don't think you're going to get out of helping me in the future!" She winked at Shelby.

Allison continued, "And I'll do a reduced board so you can work off most of it. You're out here working all the time anyways. It's only fair. I'm really excited to watch you progress with your own horse. It's going to be the start of something really exciting!"

Shelby wiped tears as she hugged Taylor. "You knew about this and you didn't tell me?" she teased her friend.

"I only found out this morning!" Taylor laughed.

"We couldn't tell her! We knew she'd tell you!" Shelby's dad joked.

A car pulled up outside and Tucker and Sage ran inside the barn.

"Hey, Shelby! You got a horse. That's so cool!" her little brother said jumping around.

Sage gave her sister a hug. "Congratulations. I'm proud of you," she whispered in Shelby's ear.

Sage looked into Gatsby's stall. "Holy cow! He looks so much better than he did! Wow, he's gorgeous, Shelby. I can't wait to photograph him."

"Can I get him out?" Shelby asked.

"Sure, silly. He's your horse," Allison responded.

Shelby's mom produced a halter that she handed to Shelby. It was a beautiful brown leather halter with a brass nameplate that read:

SGF GREAT GATSBY
SHELBY DAVIES

"It's official," Taylor said nodding at the halter. "He's all yours!"

Shelby buckled the halter on Gatsby's head and led him out of the stall. She threw her arms around his neck and buried her head in his mane. She inhaled the smell of horse... her horse, then looked up and proclaimed to her family and friends, "This is the best day ever!"

The End

About the Author

Shannon Jett realized she was a horse crazy girl after her first riding lesson for her 13th birthday. She rode on her high school's equestrian team and eventually chose her college by picking the one with the best facility for her horse! She rode for and was captain of her IHSA equestrian team in Murray, Kentucky. (Go Racers!)

Her passion has given her the opportunity to pursue many aspects of the equestrian world. Early on in her career she fell in love with the Arabian horse and had the opportunity to learn from several well-known trainers and work with talented horses. She loves the willingness and temperament of the breed as well as everything the Arabian community has to offer. Shannon also enjoyed helping many riders get their start, often enjoying their first ride and eventually their first show. She found it rewarding to help other horse crazy people develop their passion.

Shannon currently lives in Georgia with her husband, two daughters, two dogs and three horses. She enjoys writing, training her half Arabian, Stella, for the hunter ring and raising the next generation of equestrians.

Rivermont Farm

Shelby and her fellow High Lane Farm riders attend a show series called the Rivermont Silver Stirrup Series. This series is based off of a real show series run every year at Rivermont Farm in Lyerly, Georgia. Rivermont is a beautiful farm on nearly 50 acres with an incredible jump arena featuring brightly colored, fun jumps that any equestrian would be excited to sail over. The farm hosts an annual schooling show series with monthly shows from February through December. The shows have classes for hunters and jumpers and all levels of horses and riders.

Be sure to check out their website at www.rivermontfarm.com which highlights lots of neat stories and pictures of their horses, riders and horse shows. There is also information on the owner's small business, GlamourAlls, which feature stylish ladies coveralls. And, just in case you are looking, Rivermont Farm is currently for sale!

I am happy to be able to help support the following organizations that help both horses and horsemen in need. Ten percent of the proceeds of the High Lane Farm series will be split between the following two organizations that are near and dear to my heart.

Thank you for your support!

Shannon Jett

Red Clay Ranch

Red Clay Ranch Equine Rescue and Sanctuary is owned by my friend Lee Rast who is an incredibly inspirational person. In retirement, she and her husband, Phil, began to realize the desperate need for a safe place for equines in different stages of life. RCR is dedicated to the compassionate care of retired, unwanted and/or neglected equines. Their mission is to save and protect equines in need by offering them a forever home, providing them with life-long care and rehabilitation. RCR is currently the home of around 60 horses, including retirees, victims of abuse and neglect and several younger horses whose injuries prevent them from being adoptable. In recent years, the Rasts have become one of the few rescues in the area that has the appropriate facility to support and care for blind horses. They currently house and love eight blind horses.

I really can't put into words how impressive this rescue is. With just themselves, a trainer and the help of volunteers, the Rasts manage the care of around 60 horses, vast acreage and the constant needs of horses that otherwise have nowhere to turn. I can personally attest to that fact that these horses are not only so very loved, but they receive anything they need, whether it is veterinary, farrier, nutrition or training related. Lee and Phil handle each individual horse as a blessing and handle even the saddest of situations with grace and forgiveness. The horses that wind up in the care of RCR are truly blessed.

If you'd like to learn more and see how you can help, please visit their website www.redclayrescue.org or find them on Facebook to see all of the wonderful things they are doing.

Arabian Horsemen's Distress Fund

Since its establishment in 2005, the AHDF has raised and disbursed over $1,000,000 to support a wide variety of Arabian community members during times of unexpected crisis. Working strictly off of donations of all sizes from $5 on up, each donation not only assists a community member during a difficult time, but goes on to share a bit of extra courage. Courage is a trait the Arabian horse has been prized for, for over 2000 years of selective breeding and it's a trait that they share with the people who own and ride them.

Donations received by AHDF have gone on to help many Arabian community members during times of unexpected crisis. From unimaginable barn fires and catastrophic accidents, to health crises that impair the ability to meet expenses and care for family members and animals, the fund has become a vehicle that is up and ready to respond immediately when unexpected calamity strikes.

As an Arabian owner and a lover of the Arabian breed, I feel that AHDF truly represents the comradery and family environment that the Arabian community fosters. From large, well-known training barns to small time breeders with just a handful of horses, AHDF is available for anyone supporting the breed.

For more information or to make a secure donation please visit the website, www.arabianhorsemensdistressfund.com. You can also donate through Amazon Smile by noting AHDF as your charity of choice.

Made in the USA
Middletown, DE
15 November 2020